The Bird Strike

Sally Browner

Published by Bright Minds Books, 2024.

THE BIRD STRIKE

First edition. December 9, 2024.

ISBN: 979-8230296423

Written by Sally Browner.

Table of Contents

Description

The Bird Strike is a heartwarming and thought-provoking story about a flock of geese and their unexpected journey to coexist with humans.

When Greta, a wise and fearless leader, leads her flock to an airport sanctuary, she unwittingly sparks a partnership that changes everything. Against a backdrop of environmental challenges and technological innovations, humans and geese must work together to navigate their shared skies.

Full of resilience, humor, and surprising lessons, this tale explores how trust and collaboration can bridge even the widest divides. A story for all ages, *The Bird Strike* celebrates hope, leadership, and the power of unity.

Dedication

To those who dare to look up and wonder,
To the leaders who guide us through storms,
And to the quiet partnerships that make the impossible possible—
This book is for you.

Preface

The sky has always been a symbol of freedom—a vast, open space shared by birds, planes, and dreams. Yet, as human progress soars, it often clashes with the natural rhythms of wildlife.

The Bird Strike was born from this tension, inspired by real-life challenges and the hope for harmonious solutions. At its heart, this story isn't just about geese or machines; it's about the delicate balance between nature and human innovation, and the lessons we can learn from each other.

As you journey through Greta's world, may you discover the beauty of coexistence and the boundless potential of working together.

Chapter 1: The Sky is for Everyone

Captain Sarah Skylark had flown through countless sunrises and sunsets, seen storms roar and quiet, and even once spotted a cloud shaped like an elephant doing ballet. But this morning, as she strode across the tarmac of Skylark Airport with her coffee cup balanced precariously on her clipboard, something felt different. Maybe it was the way the sun seemed to linger just a second longer on the horizon, casting an orange glow on everything. Or maybe it was the distant cacophony of honks that sounded suspiciously like a marching band of disgruntled trumpets.

Skylark Airport wasn't the biggest or the fanciest, but it was home. The ground crew knew her by name, the coffee from "Cloud 9 Café" was marginally tolerable, and the view from the cockpit always managed to take her breath away. But today, there was a curious energy in the air—a kind of restlessness that had Sarah furrowing her brows.

As she reached the hangar, her first officer, Jerry, waved enthusiastically, holding a bag of peanuts. "Sarah! Did you hear about the geese?" he asked, his grin too wide for someone who had been awake since 4:30 a.m.

"Geese?" Sarah repeated, taking a sip of her coffee. "Unless they've learned to pilot planes, I'm not interested."

"Well," Jerry said, lowering his voice as though he was sharing classified information, "a whole flock of them landed by Runway 2. Dozens of them! They're just... hanging out. Like they've claimed the airport as their personal goose spa."

Sarah blinked. Geese at an airport were no joke. She'd heard the stories—engines clogged with feathers, emergency landings, chaos in the skies. But a goose invasion? That was new.

"Let's hope they've got boarding passes," Sarah muttered, heading for the control tower.

Up in the tower, the scene was a mix of organized chaos and mild panic. Controllers juggled calls from incoming planes while squinting at their radars, which seemed to flicker with tiny, moving blips.

"What's the situation?" Sarah asked, stepping inside.

One of the controllers, a lanky man named Lou, gestured toward the window. "See for yourself."

Sarah looked out and almost dropped her coffee. There, on the grassy expanse near Runway 2, was a gaggle of geese so large it looked like a feathery flash mob. They honked, flapped their wings, and waddled around as though auditioning for a reality show called *The Goose Life*.

"Well," Sarah said, after a long pause. "That's... festive."

"Festive?!" Lou exclaimed. "It's a disaster! Flight 217 had to circle twice because the geese refused to budge. One of them actually stood in front of the plane and stared it down. Stared it down, Sarah! Like a feathered vigilante!"

Sarah couldn't help but chuckle, even as she recognized the seriousness of the situation. "Okay, Lou. Relax. Let's not declare war on the geese just yet. Have we tried... I don't know, shooing them away?"

Lou threw his hands in the air. "We tried. They honked at us. Loudly. It was terrifying."

Sarah sighed, her pilot instincts kicking in. Geese weren't just a nuisance—they were a danger. But something about this particular flock seemed oddly deliberate, as though they weren't just there by accident.

Meanwhile, down by the runway, Greta, the leader of the geese, fluffed her feathers and surveyed her surroundings. Greta was no ordinary goose. She was bold, clever, and had an impressive wingspan that made her look like the Beyoncé of waterfowl. She'd led her flock here after weeks of searching for a safe landing spot. Parks were too crowded with humans. Lakes were drying up. And now this wide-open stretch of grass seemed perfect—if only the giant metal birds would stop roaring overhead.

"Alright, team," Greta honked to her flock. "We're staying put. This is our land now. Honk if you agree."

A chorus of honks erupted, echoing across the tarmac.

Back in the tower, Sarah was hatching a plan. "Jerry," she said into her radio, "get the wildlife expert down here. Tom, wasn't it? We need to figure out why these geese are so stubborn."

Tom arrived half an hour later, wearing khaki shorts, a safari hat, and an expression of profound exasperation. "Geese," he said flatly, shaking Sarah's hand. "Why is it always geese?"

"Because they're too smart for their own good," Sarah replied. "Can you move them?"

Tom sighed, producing a small device that looked like a remote control for a toy car. "I can try. This thing emits a sound that's supposed to scare birds away. Works like a charm—most of the time."

Sarah raised an eyebrow. "Most of the time?"

Tom shrugged. "Let's just say geese are... resistant."

The group headed to the field, where the geese were now lounging as if they were on vacation. Greta watched them approach with narrowed eyes.

"Oh great," she muttered. "More humans. Everyone, look intimidating."

The flock flapped their wings in unison, creating a mini windstorm. Tom pressed a button on his device, and a high-pitched noise filled the air. The geese barely flinched. Greta raised a wing and signaled for silence.

"Is that supposed to scare us?" she called out, her honk dripping with sarcasm. "Pathetic."

Sarah, who couldn't understand goose language but definitely sensed the attitude, folded her arms. "This isn't working."

"No kidding," Tom replied, fiddling with his device. "Plan B?"

"Plan B is figuring out why they're here," Sarah said, scanning the flock. She spotted Greta, who was clearly in charge. Their eyes met, and for a moment, it felt like a showdown in an old Western movie.

Greta held her ground, her feathers bristling. This was her turf now, and she wasn't about to give it up without a fight.

Back at the tower, Sarah debriefed with Jerry and Tom. "We're dealing with smart birds," she said. "We need to think outside the box."

Jerry scratched his head. "What if we... negotiate?"

Sarah snorted. "With geese?"

"Why not?" Jerry said. "Offer them something better than what they've got here. A pond, maybe. Or free snacks."

Sarah laughed, but the idea wasn't entirely absurd. "Alright," she said. "Let's figure out what they want. In the meantime, keep the planes circling and hope these geese don't organize a sit-in."

As the sun set over Skylark Airport, the geese settled in for the night, their honks growing softer. Greta gazed at the humans from her makeshift perch, wondering what they'd try next. The humans were persistent, she'd give them that. But so was she.

The sky, Greta thought, is for everyone.

Chapter 2: The Flock Arrives

The day the flock landed at Skylark Airport began like any other, except for the faint hum of tension in the air. Greta led her flock through a patchwork of low-hanging clouds, her eyes scanning the landscape below. The rolling hills they once called home had transformed into a labyrinth of highways and buildings. Lakes were no longer shimmering havens but shrinking puddles, edged with warning signs and fences.

Greta felt the weight of every wingbeat behind her. Her flock trusted her to find a safe haven, but the options were dwindling. When she saw the expanse of Skylark Airport—open fields, trimmed grass, and no immediate predators—it looked like an oasis in the desert.

"This is it," Greta honked, her voice steady and firm. She circled once, signaling the others to prepare for landing. "Spread out. Take your time. We've earned a rest."

The flock descended gracefully, wings cutting through the air like paper gliders. Greta landed first, her webbed feet touching the ground with precision. Behind her, a symphony of honks and wingbeats followed as the others joined her. They waddled onto the grassy stretch by Runway 2, a spot that felt perfectly out of the way of the metal beasts roaring nearby.

For the first time in weeks, they had space to breathe. Goslings played tag among the grass, flapping their tiny wings in delight. Older geese preened their feathers, and Greta allowed herself a moment to rest. This, she thought, might just work.

But peace didn't last long.

High above, a sleek passenger plane descended for landing, its engines rumbling like a thunderstorm. Greta snapped to attention, her instincts flaring. The roar grew louder, and before she could react, the massive machine swooped low over the flock. The wind from its engines sent feathers flying, and the goslings squealed in terror.

"Stay together!" Greta called, rallying her flock as the plane disappeared down the runway. She turned to see a young goose, Max, staring wide-eyed at the sky.

"Are they always this loud?" Max asked, trembling.

Greta nodded, her feathers ruffling. "We'll need to stay alert. They may not mean harm, but they don't see us the way we see them."

Unbeknownst to Greta, their arrival had not gone unnoticed. Back in the control tower, Lou squinted at his binoculars, his face pale. "Uh, we've got... a situation. I count at least thirty geese. Maybe more."

Jerry, who had stopped by to drop off coffee, nearly choked. "Thirty? You sure they're not just... like... spread out? Maybe it's ten, but they move a lot?"

Lou gave him a withering look. "Jerry, this isn't a picnic. That's a flock big enough to start its own airline."

Sarah arrived moments later, her face set in determined calm. "What's the status?"

Lou handed her the binoculars. "See for yourself."

Sarah peered through and immediately spotted Greta, standing tall amidst the flock. "That's the leader," she said without hesitation.

"Leader?" Jerry asked, sipping his coffee. "What are they, a motorcycle gang?"

"Every group has a leader," Sarah replied. "And that one has the look of a commander. We'll have to deal with her first."

Meanwhile, down by the runway, Greta was strategizing. The flock needed to stay calm, but it was clear that the airfield was no ordinary patch of grass. The metal beasts roared past periodically, each one louder than the last. But Greta had made up her mind—this place was their best chance for survival.

"Listen up!" Greta called, her voice cutting through the chatter. The flock gathered, forming a loose semicircle around her. "We've faced worse than this. Remember the storm over the lake? The fox in the meadow? We've survived it all, and we'll survive this. Stay together. Stay low. And whatever you do, don't panic."

Her words steadied the flock, and for a moment, they felt hopeful. But hope was fleeting, especially when a new noise filled the air—a high-pitched whine that sent a shiver down every goose's spine.

Tom had arrived with his "magical" bird deterrent device and was testing it from the edge of the field. The sound, which humans could barely hear, was designed to irritate birds enough to drive them away. Greta's flock reacted instantly, their honks rising in panic.

"Hold your ground!" Greta shouted, though her own nerves were fraying. She spread her wings, a signal for the others to stay put.

"What's she doing?" Sarah murmured from the tower, watching Greta's defiant stance.

"Being stubborn," Tom replied, adjusting the frequency of his device. "Geese are like that. You push, they push back."

Greta, however, wasn't being stubborn for stubbornness's sake. She understood that retreating now would set a dangerous precedent. If they gave up this patch of safety, where would they go next? The flock needed stability, and she would provide it.

As the high-pitched whine grew louder, Greta hatched a plan. She led the flock in a sudden, synchronized maneuver, lifting off the ground in a tight formation. They flew low and fast, circling the device before landing farther down the field. It was a move designed to confuse and frustrate the humans—and it worked.

"Did... did they just outsmart us?" Jerry asked, his coffee cup frozen mid-air.

Tom groaned. "Great. We're dealing with tactical geniuses now."

Sarah couldn't help but smile. "I told you that one's the leader."

The battle of wits continued into the afternoon. Each time the humans tried a new tactic—flashing lights, scarecrows, even a recording of a hawk's cry—the geese adapted, finding new ways to stay one step ahead. It became clear that Greta's flock wasn't just surviving—they were thriving in this strange new environment.

By sunset, the humans were exhausted, their efforts yielding little progress. Greta, on the other hand, stood triumphant, her flock gathered around her like loyal soldiers.

"We've won this day," she said softly, though she knew the fight wasn't over. The humans weren't their enemies, but they weren't allies either—not yet. For now, all that mattered was that her flock was safe.

Back in the tower, Sarah leaned against the console, her mind racing. The geese were smart, resourceful, and clearly determined to stay. Forcing them out wasn't an option, and neither was letting them stay unchecked. There had to be another way.

As the last light of day faded into twilight, Skylark Airport buzzed with activity, the tension between humans and geese simmering like a pot about to boil over. But amidst the chaos, there was an unspoken understanding—a respect, even—between the two sides. Both were fighting for survival, and neither was ready to back down.

Tomorrow, Sarah thought, would be a new day. And with it, new challenges—and maybe, just maybe, new solutions.

Chapter 3: A Close Call

The morning after the flock's arrival dawned with a peculiar stillness, a deceptive calm that hinted at the chaos to come. Captain Sarah Skylark stood at the edge of Skylark Airport's main runway, the early light glinting off her aviator sunglasses. She sipped her coffee—a brew so dark it could probably double as jet fuel—and watched the geese in the distance. They seemed peaceful enough, waddling and preening in the grass, their leader—Sarah had named her "Commander Goose" in her head—standing watch like a sentinel.

"Today will be fine," Sarah muttered to herself, though she didn't entirely believe it.

The tower buzzed with activity as the airport geared up for its busiest time of day. Flights were scheduled to arrive and depart in rapid succession, and the geese had shown no signs of leaving. Lou's voice crackled over Sarah's radio.

"Captain, we've got Flight 308 inbound, estimated touchdown in five. And... uh... the geese are still doing their thing. Just thought you'd like to know."

Sarah sighed, gripping her radio tighter. "Acknowledged, Lou. Let's keep everything running smoothly. No surprises."

But surprises, as it turned out, were in plentiful supply.

Flight 308, a commercial airliner with over a hundred passengers onboard, was descending steadily. Its pilot, Captain Marcus, was calm as he communicated with the tower. His co-pilot, a rookie named Dale, scanned the runway nervously.

"Looks clear," Dale said, though his voice wavered.

"Relax," Marcus replied. "It's just another landing. We've done this a thousand times."

But as the plane approached, something caught Dale's eye—a flicker of movement near the runway. At first, he thought it was a trick of the light, but then he saw them. Geese. Dozens of them, too close for comfort.

"Uh, Captain?" Dale said, his voice rising. "We've got company."

Marcus frowned, glancing out the cockpit window. His face tightened as he spotted the flock. "Tower, this is Flight 308. We've got birds near the runway. Repeat, birds near the runway."

In the control tower, Lou paled. "Flight 308, understood. Hold your approach. We're assessing the situation."

The radio exchange crackled through Sarah's earpiece as she sprinted toward a ground vehicle. "I'm on it," she said, climbing into the driver's seat and speeding toward the geese. The vehicle jolted over the uneven ground, and Sarah honked the horn, hoping to scatter the flock.

But Greta wasn't having it. She spread her wings wide, standing her ground as the metal beast approached. The younger geese huddled behind her, watching their leader with a mixture of awe and terror.

"Not today," Greta thought, her honk a battle cry. "We're not running again."

The vehicle slowed to a stop a few feet away, and Sarah jumped out, waving her arms. "Shoo!" she yelled, feeling slightly ridiculous. "Go on! Move!"

Greta honked back, a sound so defiant it might as well have been a declaration of war. She flapped her wings, sending a gust of air toward Sarah, who stumbled backward in surprise.

"Are you serious?" Sarah muttered, glaring at the goose. "This is not how I imagined my morning."

Back in the air, Marcus was growing uneasy. "Tower, we're running low on options here. I can't keep circling forever."

Lou's voice was strained. "Understood, Flight 308. Hold your position. Ground team is... working on it."

"Working on it?" Marcus echoed, his grip tightening on the controls. "Not exactly reassuring."

Dale, meanwhile, was transfixed by the scene below. "Look at that goose," he murmured. "She's... fearless."

Marcus shot him a look. "We don't have time to admire the wildlife, Dale."

On the ground, Sarah was losing patience. She grabbed a blanket from the back of the vehicle and began waving it like a matador. Greta tilted her head, unimpressed.

"Is she trying to start a fight?" Greta wondered, her feathers ruffling. "Bold move, human."

The stalemate was broken by a sudden noise—a deafening roar as Flight 308's engines grew closer. Greta turned, her sharp eyes locking onto the approaching plane. It was coming in too low, too fast. The flock panicked, scattering in all directions.

Sarah's heart lurched as she realized the danger. "No, no, no!" she yelled, scrambling back into the vehicle. She slammed on the horn, hoping to drive the remaining geese away.

In the cockpit, Marcus made a split-second decision. "We're aborting," he said, pulling up the nose of the plane. The aircraft roared past the runway, its shadow sweeping over the field below.

The tower erupted into chaos as controllers scrambled to adjust the schedule. Lou's voice cracked over the radio. "Flight 308, proceed to holding pattern. We'll sort this out."

Marcus exhaled, his knuckles white on the controls. "Holding pattern," he muttered. "Great."

On the ground, Sarah watched the plane disappear into the sky, her heart pounding. She turned to see Greta still standing in the middle of the field, her flock regrouping around her.

"You've got guts," Sarah said aloud, though she knew the goose couldn't understand. "But this isn't a game. People's lives are at stake."

Greta stared back, unflinching. For a moment, Sarah felt an odd connection to the bird—an understanding that both of them were just trying to protect what mattered most.

The aftermath of the near-miss was swift and intense. News of the incident spread quickly, with headlines proclaiming everything from "Airport Chaos: Geese Take Over" to "Feathered Foes Ground Planes." Reporters swarmed Skylark Airport, and Sarah found herself at the center of a media storm.

"What's being done to prevent future incidents?" one journalist asked, shoving a microphone in her face.

Sarah forced a smile. "We're working closely with wildlife experts to ensure safety for both planes and birds. It's a complex situation, but we're committed to finding a solution."

Behind the scenes, however, tensions were high. The airport's board of directors demanded immediate action, and Tom was brought in for an emergency meeting.

"These geese are a problem," one board member said, pounding the table. "We need them gone—now."

Tom frowned. "With all due respect, forcing them out isn't a long-term solution. We need to address why they're here in the first place."

"And what do you suggest?" another member snapped. "Building them a five-star hotel?"

Sarah stepped in. "Tom's right. This isn't just about moving them—it's about understanding them. They're not here by choice. Something pushed them to this point."

The board was skeptical, but Sarah's determination won them over—for now. A temporary halt on flights was implemented, giving the team time to assess the situation.

Meanwhile, Greta held her own emergency meeting. The flock was rattled by the close call, and murmurs of dissent rippled through the group.

"We can't stay here," one goose said. "It's too dangerous."

"And go where?" Greta shot back. "This is the safest place we've found. We just need to be smarter."

"But what if they come back?" Max asked, his voice trembling.

Greta hesitated, her usual confidence faltering. She had always prided herself on keeping the flock safe, but today's events had shaken her. Still, she refused to give up. Not yet.

"We stay," she said firmly, her gaze sweeping over the flock. "But we'll be ready. Next time, we won't just survive—we'll thrive."

Chapter 4: Greta's Perspective

Greta stood on the edge of the grassy field, the faint hum of distant engines vibrating through the ground beneath her feet. The flock was quiet for now, some huddling together for comfort while others groomed their feathers in a display of forced normalcy. But Greta knew the truth. Their close call with the metal beast had shaken them to their cores.

She turned her head slowly, scanning the horizon. The setting sun painted the sky with hues of orange and pink, casting long shadows over Skylark Airport. Greta's sharp eyes caught every detail—the swaying blades of grass, the movement of distant vehicles, and the imposing shapes of the planes lined up near the terminal. She could feel the tension in the air, as if the very atmosphere braced itself for the next clash.

It hadn't always been this way. Greta's life had once been filled with tranquil migrations, the steady rhythm of wingbeats carrying her flock across vast landscapes. They would follow rivers and lakes, navigating by the stars, always returning to the familiar comforts of home. But home was gone now, swallowed up by human expansion. The lakes had shrunk to mere puddles, and the wetlands were paved over, leaving her flock with fewer and fewer places to rest.

Greta ruffled her feathers, a habitual gesture she used to mask her worry. As the leader of the flock, it was her responsibility to remain strong, even when the odds were against them. She glanced over at Max, a young goose who had taken to shadowing her ever since they left their last nesting ground. He was watching her now, his wide eyes full of questions he didn't dare ask.

"Go join the others, Max," Greta said gently, nodding toward the flock. "You need to rest."

"But what if it happens again?" Max whispered, his voice barely audible. "What if the big metal bird comes back?"

Greta sighed, her heart aching for the gosling's innocence. "If it comes back, we'll face it together. That's what we do. We protect each other."

Max hesitated, then nodded and shuffled off to join the others. Greta watched him go, her mind racing. How could she protect them when the danger was unlike anything they'd faced before? Predators she could handle, storms she could outfly, but these machines were relentless, their power unmatched.

She looked back at the airport, where the humans were bustling about. They were fascinating creatures, with their strange machines and loud voices. Greta had seen humans before, but never this close. They seemed to move with purpose, always rushing from one task to the next. Yet there was something almost comical about them, too—like the woman who had waved a blanket at them earlier, as if trying to shoo away a swarm of flies. Greta had to admit, it had been amusing.

But amusement wasn't enough to distract her from the reality of their situation. The flock couldn't stay here forever, not with the constant threat of the metal birds. Yet leaving was just as risky. Every direction held uncertainty—more humans, more machines, more obstacles. Greta's instincts told her to stay, to hold her ground and find a way to coexist with these strange creatures. But her instincts also warned her that the humans might not see things the same way.

As the sun dipped lower, casting the airport in shadow, Greta called the flock together. They gathered around her in a loose circle, their murmurs quieting as they waited for her to speak. She took a deep breath, steeling herself.

"We've faced challenges before," Greta began, her voice steady. "We've outsmarted foxes, weathered storms, and found food in the harshest winters. This is no different. Yes, these metal birds are powerful, but they're not invincible. And neither are the humans who control them."

A few of the older geese exchanged skeptical glances. One of them, a gray-feathered gander named Horace, spoke up. "And what do you suggest we do, Greta? Fight them? They're not like foxes. They don't run when you honk at them."

Greta met his gaze, refusing to back down. "No, they don't. But they're not our enemies, either. I've been watching them, and I think they're trying to figure out what to do about us, just as we're trying to figure out what to do about them."

"So what? We sit here and wait for them to make the first move?" Horace pressed.

"We stay alert," Greta replied firmly. "We adapt. If they push, we push back. But we don't give up this ground. Not yet."

The murmurs grew louder as the flock debated her words. Some agreed with her, while others argued that staying put was too dangerous. Greta listened patiently, letting them voice their concerns. She knew she couldn't force them to follow her—leadership wasn't about commands; it was about trust.

Finally, Max spoke up, his voice small but resolute. "I think Greta's right. We've been running for too long. If we leave now, we'll just have to start over somewhere else. At least here, we have a chance to figure things out."

His words seemed to strike a chord with the others, and the murmurs began to die down. Greta nodded, grateful for his support. "We'll take it one day at a time," she said. "But remember, we're strongest when we work together. If we're careful and smart, we can make this work."

As the flock dispersed to rest, Greta remained where she was, gazing up at the stars that had begun to appear in the darkening sky. She thought about the humans, wondering what they were doing at that very moment. Were they as worried as she was? Did they have leaders, too? And if so, what kind of leader was the woman who had faced her earlier? There had been something different about her—something determined yet kind.

Greta shook her head, dismissing the thought. Humans and geese might share the same sky, but they lived in different worlds. Still, she couldn't shake the feeling that their fates were now intertwined, whether they liked it or not.

Back at the control tower, Sarah sat with a steaming cup of coffee, staring at the radar screen. The geese were still there, their presence a constant blip on the airport's operations. She thought about the lead goose—the one who had stood her ground despite the chaos around her. There was something about that bird that reminded Sarah of herself: stubborn, resourceful, unwilling to back down.

"Commander Goose," Sarah murmured with a wry smile. "What's your next move?"

She didn't have an answer, but she knew one thing for certain: the geese weren't going anywhere anytime soon. And neither was she.

Chapter 5: The Big Meeting

The conference room at Skylark Airport was filled to capacity. The tension was as thick as the coffee being served, which, according to Jerry, could dissolve a spoon if left unattended. Sarah leaned against the wall, arms crossed, surveying the mix of airport officials, wildlife experts, and aviation regulators seated around the long table. They looked like a group preparing for battle, which, in a way, they were.

"This isn't just about a few geese," boomed Roger Timmons, the airport's operations manager, slamming his clipboard onto the table. His voice had the gravelly edge of a man who smoked cigars the size of hockey sticks. "This is about safety. About reputation. We can't have planes dodging birds like we're running some sort of aerial obstacle course."

"I understand your concerns, Roger," Sarah said, keeping her tone even, though she wanted to roll her eyes. "But this isn't just a PR issue. It's an ecological one, too. Those geese didn't pick Skylark Airport because they wanted a vacation. They're here because their habitat is disappearing."

Tom, the airport's wildlife expert, nodded. "Sarah's right. This isn't a random occurrence. It's a pattern we've been seeing for years. Urban sprawl, shrinking wetlands—these geese are out of options."

"Well, they need to find new options!" Roger barked. "Preferably far away from my runways."

Sarah took a deep breath. "And how do you propose we make that happen? Blast them into the next county? Because that's not a solution—it's a temporary fix that creates more problems down the line."

"Okay, let's all take a breath," interjected Lisa Patel, the meeting's moderator. She was an environmental liaison who seemed to possess infinite patience, though Sarah suspected even Lisa's composure had limits. "We're here to find solutions, not trade barbs."

Roger grumbled but sank back into his chair, muttering something about "bird sympathizers."

"Let's look at the facts," Lisa continued, clicking a remote to bring up a slideshow on the screen. The first image was a satellite view of the region, showing the airport surrounded by a patchwork of urban development and sparse green spaces. "As you can see, the geese are reacting to habitat loss. Skylark Airport represents one of the last open areas in their migration path. We can't expect them to leave without offering a viable alternative."

"What kind of alternative are we talking about?" asked Donna, a representative from the aviation safety board. "Because I'm not sure the airlines are going to wait while we build a goose playground."

Tom raised a hand. "Actually, there are some proven methods we can implement. Decoy habitats, for example. If we create a wetland nearby, complete with food sources and shelter, the geese might naturally relocate."

"'Might'?" Roger pounced on the word like a cat on a mouse. "We can't operate on 'might.' We need guarantees."

Sarah interjected, her voice firm. "Roger, there are no guarantees. But what we do know is that scaring them off isn't working. We've tried noise, lights, even predator calls. These geese are smart, and they're not going anywhere unless we give them a better option."

Lisa nodded in agreement. "It's clear we need a long-term strategy that balances safety with environmental responsibility. Tom, can you draft a proposal for creating a nearby sanctuary?"

Tom looked hesitant. "I can, but it'll require funding and cooperation from local governments. This isn't something we can whip up overnight."

"And in the meantime?" Donna asked. "Planes are still flying, and those geese are still there."

Sarah spoke up again. "We need a temporary plan. Something to minimize risks while we work on the sanctuary."

“Like what?” Roger asked, his tone dripping with skepticism. “Handing out goose traffic cones?”

Sarah ignored the jab. “We could implement adjusted flight paths, at least during peak migration times. It’s not perfect, but it reduces the chance of a collision.”

The room fell silent as everyone considered her suggestion. Adjusting flight paths was a logistical headache, but it was better than dealing with the aftermath of a bird strike.

“Alright,” Lisa said finally. “We’ll split this into two phases. Tom, you’ll head the sanctuary proposal. Sarah, work with air traffic control on temporary flight adjustments. Let’s reconvene next week to assess progress.”

The meeting ended with a mix of cautious optimism and lingering frustration. As the attendees filed out, Sarah caught Tom’s eye.

“Do you think this will work?” she asked quietly.

Tom shrugged. “It’s worth a shot. These geese aren’t going to make it easy, though.”

Sarah smiled faintly. “Neither am I.”

Meanwhile, back on the field, Greta was holding her own meeting. The flock had gathered in a tight circle, their murmurs of concern filling the air. Greta stood in the center, her posture commanding.

“We’ve made it this far,” she began, her voice strong. “But the humans aren’t happy. They want us gone.”

“What do they want from us?” grumbled Horace, the older gander. “We’re not hurting anyone.”

“Not intentionally,” Greta replied. “But their metal birds can’t fly if we’re in the way. And we can’t stay here if they keep trying to scare us off.”

“So what do we do?” asked Max, his eyes wide.

“We adapt,” Greta said firmly. “We stay vigilant, we move when we have to, and we don’t let them push us around.”

The flock exchanged uneasy glances. Greta knew they were tired, frustrated, and scared. But she also knew they trusted her. She had led them through storms and predators; she could lead them through this.

"We're not just surviving," Greta continued, her voice rising. "We're proving that we belong here. This is our home now, and we're not giving it up."

A ripple of agreement passed through the flock. Max straightened up, his small chest puffing with determination. Even Horace nodded, though his expression remained skeptical.

As the flock dispersed, Greta stayed behind, her mind racing with thoughts of the humans. She didn't understand their language, but she had watched them closely. The woman who had faced her earlier—the one with the strong voice and sharp eyes—was different from the others. Greta couldn't shake the feeling that this human was trying to solve the problem, not just chase them away.

For now, though, Greta focused on her flock. They needed her strength, and she would not let them down.

Back in her office, Sarah stared at the sanctuary proposal Tom had emailed her. It was a good plan, ambitious but feasible. Yet she couldn't shake the feeling that the geese weren't just a problem to be solved—they were something more.

She glanced out the window, where the flock was huddled on the grass. Her eyes found the leader, standing tall and alert. "Commander Goose," she murmured with a wry smile. "What's your next move?"

The question hung in the air, unanswered but full of possibilities.

Chapter 6: Trouble in the Sky

The morning began with the sort of deceptive calm that usually preceded chaos. The air was crisp, the runway lights gleamed against the pale dawn, and the flock of geese grazed peacefully in their makeshift territory. For a fleeting moment, Skylark Airport seemed to hold its breath, teetering on the edge of tranquility. Then, without warning, the hum of trouble began to build—first faint, then unmistakable.

In the control tower, Lou sipped his coffee as the radar blinked steadily. Everything looked routine until it didn't. A new blip appeared, moving rapidly toward the airport. He leaned closer, narrowing his eyes.

"Unscheduled approach," Lou muttered into his headset. "Tower to unidentified aircraft, state your call sign and intentions."

Static answered him. Frowning, Lou repeated the message, his voice firmer this time.

"Still nothing?" Sarah asked, striding into the tower. She had a sixth sense for trouble and, unfortunately for Lou, it rarely failed.

Lou shook his head. "They're not responding. Looks like a private plane, coming in fast."

Sarah grabbed a pair of binoculars and scanned the horizon. The glint of the incoming aircraft was unmistakable—a small twin-engine plane descending erratically.

"Great," she muttered. "That's all we need. Let's try to get them on the ground safely. Any word from the geese?"

Lou glanced out the window, his expression grim. "They're still out there. This is going to be tight."

Down on the field, Greta's feathers ruffled as she sensed the disturbance in the air. She didn't need to see the approaching plane to know it was trouble; the vibrations in the ground told her everything. She honked sharply, rallying her flock.

"Something's coming," she warned. "Stay alert!"

The geese responded with a flurry of movement, clustering together and casting nervous glances skyward. Greta's sharp eyes caught sight of the plane as it descended, its engines sputtering unevenly. It was flying too low, too fast.

"This isn't right," Greta murmured, her heart pounding.

As the plane drew closer, its shadow passed over the field, sending a ripple of panic through the flock. Goslings squealed, older geese flapped their wings, and chaos erupted. Greta acted quickly, her voice cutting through the noise.

"Move! Everyone, to the far side of the field!" she commanded, leading the charge.

In the tower, Sarah watched in horror as the plane veered dangerously close to the ground. "It's losing altitude," she said, her voice tight. "Lou, get emergency services ready. This could be a hard landing."

"Already on it," Lou replied, his fingers flying across the keyboard.

The plane dipped lower, its landing gear scraping the edge of the grass. A sudden gust of wind sent it wobbling, and for a moment, it seemed as though disaster was inevitable. But the pilot managed to level out just enough to avoid catastrophe, touching down with a bone-jarring thud.

"Flight 217 is down," Lou confirmed, exhaling sharply. "No visible flames, but they're way off the runway."

"Let's get to them," Sarah said, already heading for the door.

As the emergency crews raced toward the downed plane, the geese watched from their new position at the far edge of the field. Greta's keen gaze followed the humans, her mind racing. The metal bird had come dangerously close to their territory, and she couldn't ignore the implications.

"They don't know how to share," Horace grumbled, shaking his head. "These humans think they own the sky."

"They don't own it," Greta said firmly. "But they're not going to make this easy for us. We need to be smarter."

Max, who had been unusually quiet, piped up. "Do you think they'll try to blame us for this?"

Greta hesitated. "Maybe. But that doesn't change the fact that we're here to stay. We just have to stay out of their way—for now."

At the crash site, Sarah approached the pilot, who was already out of the plane and leaning against the fuselage, looking shaken but unhurt.

"Rough landing," Sarah said, her tone brisk but not unkind. "You alright?"

The pilot nodded. "Yeah. Mechanical failure. Lost control on the approach."

Sarah scanned the area. The plane had torn through a patch of grass before coming to a stop near the perimeter fence. It was a miracle no one—human or goose—had been hurt.

"You're lucky," she said. "This could have been much worse."

The pilot gave her a weak smile. "Tell me about it."

Back in the tower, the incident sparked a flurry of activity. Reports were filed, safety protocols reviewed, and tensions simmered as everyone grappled with the close call. Roger Timmons was particularly agitated, pacing the room like a caged tiger.

"This is exactly what I was talking about!" he fumed. "We can't keep playing nice with those geese. They're a liability."

"They weren't the problem this time," Sarah countered. "The plane had mechanical issues."

"Doesn't matter," Roger snapped. "They're still a risk. If we don't get rid of them, it's only a matter of time before something worse happens."

Sarah bit back a retort, knowing it wouldn't help. Instead, she turned to Lisa, who had arrived midway through the commotion.

“Any updates on the sanctuary plan?” Sarah asked, hoping for good news.

Lisa sighed. “We’re making progress, but it’s slow. Securing funding and land takes time.”

“Well, time isn’t something we have,” Roger interjected. “If you ask me, the sanctuary’s a waste. Just relocate the geese and be done with it.”

“That’s not a solution,” Sarah said, her frustration evident. “They’ll just come back—or end up somewhere worse.”

Lisa held up a hand. “Let’s stay focused. The sanctuary is still our best long-term option, but we need immediate measures to prevent incidents like this. Sarah, can you coordinate with air traffic control to refine the flight adjustments?”

“Already on it,” Sarah replied.

Roger muttered something under his breath, but Lisa silenced him with a pointed look. “This is a team effort, Roger. Let’s keep it that way.”

As the humans scrambled to address the aftermath of the emergency landing, Greta convened her flock once more. The incident had shaken them, but it had also reinforced her resolve. They couldn’t afford to be passive; they needed to be proactive.

“We need to learn their patterns,” Greta said, addressing the group. “When their metal birds come and go, where they land, how they move. The more we know, the safer we’ll be.”

“And what do we do with that information?” Horace asked, his tone skeptical.

“We use it to adapt,” Greta replied. “If we can avoid their busiest times, we’ll reduce the risk of another close call.”

The flock murmured their agreement, and Greta felt a spark of hope. They might not have the humans’ machines or tools, but they had something just as valuable: the ability to adapt.

Chapter 7: Research Takes Flight

The morning air buzzed with quiet determination at Skylark Airport. The tension from the emergency landing still lingered, but Sarah Skylark had no time for it to fester. A solution was out there, and if the humans and geese were to share the skies peacefully, it would take more than makeshift measures and crossed fingers. It would take research, collaboration, and a little ingenuity.

Sarah stood at the airport's operations center, her coffee steaming in one hand and a clipboard in the other. Around her, a small team of wildlife experts, engineers, and air traffic controllers had gathered. Tom, the airport's resident wildlife expert, was already elbow-deep in charts and data, his khaki shirt rumpled but his focus sharp.

"Alright, everyone," Sarah began, tapping her pen on the clipboard to get their attention. "We've got a unique situation here. These geese aren't just a nuisance—they're a community. They're smart, resourceful, and they're not leaving unless we give them a better option. Our job is to figure out how we can coexist without compromising safety."

Tom nodded, pushing a map toward the center of the table. It showed the airport and its surrounding areas, with key points marked in red. "First step is understanding their behavior," he said. "We know they're migratory, but their patterns have been disrupted. What we need to figure out is why they chose Skylark Airport specifically."

"Isn't it obvious?" Roger Timmons, the airport's operations manager, grumbled from his corner of the room. "We've got wide-open fields and no predators. It's like a goose country club."

Sarah gave him a pointed look. "It's more than that, Roger. These birds are here because their natural habitats are disappearing. If we can understand what they need, we might be able to guide them to a safer location."

Lisa Patel, the environmental liaison, chimed in. "Tom and I have been reviewing data on wetland loss in the region. It's staggering. Over the last decade, we've seen a 40% decrease in suitable habitats. Skylark Airport isn't their first choice—it's their last resort."

The room fell silent as the weight of the problem settled over the team. Sarah broke the silence with a determined nod. "Alright. Let's get to work. Tom, you're on field observations. Figure out their routines, flight patterns, and feeding habits. Lisa, keep working on the sanctuary proposal. We need concrete plans to present to the board. And I'll coordinate with air traffic control to refine flight adjustments."

The team dispersed, each member diving into their tasks with renewed focus. Sarah stayed behind, staring at the map and wondering if the solution was closer than they realized.

Meanwhile, Greta was conducting her own research. The flock's near-miss with the metal bird had shaken her, but it had also sharpened her resolve. If they were going to stay at Skylark Airport, they needed to understand the humans as much as the humans were trying to understand them.

Greta perched on a small mound of grass, watching the strange machines and bustling humans in the distance. Max joined her, his youthful curiosity as bright as ever.

"What are they doing now?" Max asked, tilting his head.

"Studying us," Greta replied. "Just as we're studying them."

"Do you think they'll try to move us again?" Max's voice held a mix of fear and hope.

"Probably," Greta said honestly. "But we won't make it easy for them."

Max nodded, his small chest puffing out with newfound determination. Greta smiled slightly, impressed by his growing bravery.

"Watch closely, Max," she said. "The more we know, the better we can protect ourselves."

Tom spent the next several days immersed in his research. Armed with binoculars, a notebook, and a seemingly endless supply of granola bars, he observed the geese from a safe distance. He noted their feeding patterns, their flight times, and their interactions with one another. Greta's leadership was immediately apparent. She was always at the forefront, her sharp honks rallying the flock whenever danger approached.

"She's like a general," Tom muttered to himself as he scribbled notes. "Smart, strategic, and not afraid to take risks."

His observations weren't limited to the geese. Tom also studied the areas surrounding the airport, searching for potential sites for the sanctuary. He found a promising location a few miles away—an abandoned quarry that had naturally filled with water over the years. With a little work, it could become a perfect wetland for the geese.

Excited, Tom presented his findings at the next team meeting. "The quarry has everything the geese need," he explained, pointing to photos of the site. "It's secluded, has plenty of water, and enough space for them to thrive. If we can get the funding to restore it, I'm confident they'll move there willingly."

Lisa nodded, already jotting down notes. "I'll reach out to local conservation groups. They might be willing to help with funding and resources."

Roger, predictably, was less enthusiastic. "Even if it works, it'll take months to set up. What do we do in the meantime?"

Sarah leaned forward, her gaze steady. "We keep adapting. Tom's research gives us a better understanding of the geese. Now we can use that to refine our flight schedules and minimize conflicts."

Roger muttered something under his breath but didn't argue further. The plan was far from perfect, but it was the best option they had.

As the humans worked tirelessly to implement their plans, Greta began noticing changes. The metal birds seemed to fly at different times now, and the humans spent more time observing than chasing. It was a subtle shift, but it didn't go unnoticed by the flock.

"Do you think they're giving up?" Horace asked one evening as the flock gathered for their nightly rest.

"No," Greta replied, her tone thoughtful. "I think they're learning. Just as we are."

Max, ever the optimist, piped up. "Maybe they're trying to help us!"

"Maybe," Greta said, though she wasn't entirely convinced. Humans were unpredictable, and trust was a luxury she couldn't afford.

Still, she couldn't ignore the signs of progress. The humans seemed less hostile now, more curious than threatening. It was a small victory, but a victory nonetheless.

Weeks passed, and the collaboration between humans and geese began to show results. Tom's research informed new safety protocols, including adjusted flight paths and improved communication between pilots and ground crews. The geese, meanwhile, adapted to the humans' schedules, avoiding the runways during peak hours.

The sanctuary project gained momentum, with local conservation groups rallying behind the cause. Volunteers began clearing debris from the quarry, planting native vegetation, and building nesting areas for the geese. It was a massive undertaking, but the progress was undeniable.

For the first time in months, Skylark Airport felt a glimmer of hope. The sky was still far from peaceful, but it was no longer a battlefield.

Chapter 8: The Birds' Struggle

The days were growing shorter, and the air had a bite that hinted at the coming winter. For Greta and her flock, the struggle for survival was becoming more urgent. Despite their adaptability, the challenges of staying in the airport's shadow were mounting, and Greta could sense the growing unease among the geese.

She took a deep breath, her sharp eyes scanning for any signs of the humans' strange machines. For the moment, the skies were quiet, but she knew better than to trust the calm. The humans had been less aggressive lately, but that didn't mean the danger had disappeared. If anything, it felt like the calm before a storm.

Max waddled up beside her, his youthful energy undeterred by the chilly morning. "What's the plan today, Greta?" he asked, his eyes wide with curiosity.

Greta ruffled her feathers thoughtfully. "The plan is to stay vigilant. The humans are still watching us, and we need to stay one step ahead."

Max tilted his head. "Do you think they're really trying to help us?"

Greta hesitated. She wanted to believe the humans had good intentions—after all, they hadn't chased the flock off in weeks—but she couldn't afford to be naïve. Trusting humans too soon could put the entire flock in danger.

"They might be," she said carefully. "But it doesn't mean we can let our guard down."

Max nodded solemnly, his youthful optimism tempered by Greta's caution. He scurried off to join the others, leaving Greta alone with her thoughts.

Across the field, Tom crouched behind a cluster of tall grass, his binoculars trained on the flock. He had spent countless hours observing their behavior, and he couldn't help but admire their resilience. The geese were incredibly resourceful, finding food in the most unlikely places and navigating the complexities of the airport with surprising precision.

But even as he marveled at their adaptability, Tom couldn't ignore the signs of strain. The flock was growing thinner, their movements slower. The scarcity of food and the constant stress of living in a high-traffic area were taking their toll.

Tom scribbled a note in his journal: *Flock showing signs of fatigue. Need to expedite sanctuary plans.*

He glanced toward the quarry, where volunteers were working tirelessly to transform the barren site into a safe haven for the geese. It was coming together faster than expected, but not fast enough. The geese needed relief now, not weeks from now.

For the flock, every day felt like a new battle. The grassy field that had seemed like a sanctuary at first was proving to be a double-edged sword. The constant hum of engines and the unpredictable comings and goings of the humans' machines made it impossible to relax. Even feeding had become a challenge, as the sparse grass offered little nourishment.

"Greta, we can't keep doing this," Horace grumbled one evening as the flock gathered for their nightly rest. His voice was heavy with frustration. "We're starving, and the humans aren't going to stop their machines just because we're in the way."

Greta met his gaze, her own frustration simmering just beneath the surface. "I know it's hard, Horace. But this is the best chance we've got right now. If we leave, we risk flying into even greater danger."

"And if we stay?" Horace shot back. "What happens when the humans decide they've had enough of us?"

Greta didn't have an answer. The truth was, she wasn't sure how much longer the flock could endure. But as their leader, she couldn't afford to show doubt. Instead, she squared her shoulders and spoke with conviction.

"We'll adapt," she said firmly. "We always do."

While the geese grappled with their struggles, the humans were facing challenges of their own. At the control tower, Sarah Skylark pored over a map of the region, her coffee growing cold beside her. The sanctuary plans were progressing, but not quickly enough. Every day the geese remained at Skylark Airport was another day the risk of a collision grew.

"Any updates on the quarry?" she asked Lisa, who had joined her to review the latest reports.

Lisa sighed, pushing a strand of hair behind her ear. "The volunteers are doing everything they can, but it's slow going. Restoring a wetland isn't exactly a weekend project."

Sarah frowned, her frustration mounting. "We need to buy more time. Tom's research has been invaluable, but it's not enough. The geese are struggling, and it's only a matter of time before something gives."

Lisa nodded, her expression grim. "I'll see if we can bring in more resources. Maybe a local conservation group can help speed things along."

As Lisa left, Sarah leaned back in her chair, rubbing her temples. She felt the weight of the situation pressing down on her, but she refused to give up. There had to be a way to make this work.

Meanwhile, Greta was leading the flock on a scouting mission. The geese had ventured to the far end of the airport, where a small drainage ditch offered a meager supply of water. It wasn't much, but it was better than nothing.

"Stay close," Greta instructed, her sharp eyes scanning for any signs of danger. The flock obeyed, their movements cautious as they drank from the shallow pool.

But their respite was short-lived. The distant roar of an approaching plane sent a ripple of panic through the group. Greta acted quickly, rallying the flock and leading them back toward their usual territory. The plane roared overhead, its shadow passing over them like a predator's.

Once they were safely back in the grass, Greta took a moment to catch her breath. The constant interruptions, the dwindling resources, the unrelenting pressure—it was all starting to feel like too much.

"Greta?" Max's small voice pulled her from her thoughts. He looked up at her with wide, worried eyes. "Are we going to be okay?"

Greta hesitated, her heart aching for the young goose. She wanted to reassure him, to tell him everything would be fine. But she couldn't bring herself to lie.

"We'll do our best," she said finally. "That's all we can do."

As the days passed, the struggles of both the geese and the humans reached a breaking point. The flock grew weaker, their movements slower. The humans grew more frustrated, their tempers shorter. It seemed as though the gap between their worlds was widening, not closing.

But amidst the tension, there were moments of connection. Tom continued his observations, his respect for the geese growing with each passing day. Sarah found herself watching the flock more often, marveling at their resilience. Even Greta, despite her distrust of humans, began to sense a shift in their behavior.

Chapter 9: A Clever Solution

The early morning light cast a golden hue across Skylark Airport, but the mood among the humans and geese remained heavy with tension. Both sides had reached a breaking point, their coexistence teetering on the edge of chaos. Yet amidst the growing despair, Sarah Skylark had an idea—one so unconventional that it just might work.

Sarah stood at the operations center, tapping her pen against a map of the airport. Her team of experts and volunteers surrounded her, their faces weary but determined.

"Alright, everyone," Sarah began, her voice steady. "We've been approaching this problem from the wrong angle. The geese aren't just a hazard; they're a part of this environment now. Instead of trying to move them or scare them off, we need to create a system that lets us work with them."

Roger Timmons raised an eyebrow, his skepticism as sharp as ever. "And how exactly do you propose we do that? Teach them air traffic control?"

Sarah smirked. "Not quite, Roger. But we can teach them patterns—predictable routines that allow us to share this space without collisions."

Tom, the wildlife expert, leaned forward, his interest piqued. "You're talking about conditioned behavior. Training the geese to avoid certain areas at specific times?"

"Exactly," Sarah said. "If we can establish consistent feeding zones and rest areas for the geese away from the runways, and enforce it with gentle deterrents when necessary, they'll learn where it's safe to go."

Lisa Patel nodded thoughtfully. "That could work. Animals are incredibly adaptable, especially when food is involved. If we provide a reliable food source in the designated areas, they'll naturally gravitate there."

Roger crossed his arms, his skepticism undeterred. "And what happens when they decide they like the runways better?"

"That's where the deterrents come in," Sarah explained. "We use non-invasive methods—sounds, lights, even reflective surfaces—to discourage them from wandering into high-risk zones. It's not about forcing them out; it's about guiding them."

The room buzzed with cautious optimism as the team discussed the logistics. Tom volunteered to oversee the setup of the feeding zones, while Lisa worked on sourcing materials for the deterrents. Sarah's idea wasn't without its challenges, but for the first time in weeks, it felt like they were moving toward a real solution.

On the other side of the airport, Greta was deep in thought. The flock's struggles had weighed heavily on her, and she knew they couldn't continue like this. Despite her mistrust of humans, she had noticed their behavior changing. They weren't as aggressive now; their machines were quieter, their movements less threatening. It was as if they were trying to communicate.

"What's on your mind, Greta?" Max asked, waddling up to her side. The young goose had become her shadow, always eager to learn.

"I'm trying to figure out what the humans want," Greta replied. "They're not chasing us away anymore, but that doesn't mean they've given up."

"Maybe they're trying to help," Max suggested. His youthful optimism was both endearing and frustrating.

"Maybe," Greta said, though she wasn't convinced. "But we can't rely on them. We have to find our own way."

Over the next several days, the humans began implementing Sarah's plan. Tom and his team set up feeding stations in a quiet corner of the airport, far from the runways. They used birdseed and aquatic plants to mimic the geese's natural diet, creating an area that felt safe and familiar.

At the same time, Lisa coordinated the installation of deterrents around the high-risk zones. Reflective strips fluttered in the wind, creating a visual barrier, while soft, irregular sounds played intermittently to gently discourage the geese from venturing too close to the runways.

The changes didn't go unnoticed by the flock. Greta watched warily as the humans worked, her sharp mind analyzing their every move.

"They're up to something," Horace muttered, his feathers bristling. "We should stay away."

Greta tilted her head, considering his words. "Maybe. But we should also see what they're doing. If it's a trap, we need to know how to avoid it."

With that, Greta led a small group of geese to investigate the new feeding zones. What they found surprised her. The area was quiet, the food abundant, and there were no signs of danger. Greta pecked cautiously at the birdseed, her instincts on high alert. When nothing happened, she allowed herself a small sigh of relief.

"It's safe," she announced to the others. "For now."

The humans watched with bated breath as the geese began using the designated zones. It wasn't perfect—some geese still wandered too close to the runways, and the deterrents needed constant adjustment—but it was progress.

"They're learning," Tom observed one afternoon as he watched the flock through his binoculars. "Slowly, but they're learning."

Sarah nodded, a faint smile tugging at her lips. "So are we."

The weeks that followed were a delicate dance of adaptation and compromise. The geese grew accustomed to their new feeding zones, and the humans refined their strategies to keep the runways clear. It wasn't always smooth—there were still close calls and moments of frustration—but the system was working.

For Greta, the changes brought a mix of relief and uncertainty. The new feeding zones made life easier for the flock, but she couldn't shake the feeling that they were being manipulated. Still, she couldn't deny the results. The flock was stronger now, their movements more confident. For the first time in months, they had a semblance of stability.

"What do you think, Greta?" Max asked one evening as they rested near the feeding zone. "Are the humans really trying to help?"

Greta glanced at the young goose, her expression thoughtful. "I think they're trying to protect themselves. But if it helps us too, then maybe it doesn't matter."

The success of Sarah's plan didn't go unnoticed. Word spread about Skylark Airport's innovative approach to managing wildlife conflicts, and other airports began reaching out for advice. Sarah, Tom, and Lisa found themselves at the forefront of a movement, their work inspiring change on a larger scale.

Chapter 10: Bird vs. Machine

The sky over Skylark Airport was a battle zone again, but this time it wasn't the humans and geese in conflict—it was the relentless forces of nature and machine against a fragile harmony.

It started with a routine morning, as most disruptions often did. Captain Sarah Skylark stood in the control tower with her coffee in hand, scanning the radar. The geese were behaving, keeping to their designated zones, and for once, air traffic was smooth. She dared to think they might have turned a corner.

"Another quiet morning," Lou said, leaning back in his chair. "I don't know if it's the feeding stations or the reflective tape, but it's working."

Sarah smiled. "Don't jinx it."

Her smile faded when a new blip appeared on the radar. It was fast, erratic, and headed straight for Skylark. Lou straightened immediately, his fingers flying across the keyboard.

"Unidentified aircraft, approaching runway one-seven. This is Skylark Tower. State your call sign and intentions."

Static crackled over the radio before a garbled response came through. "This is Bravo Lima Zero Nine. Experiencing mechanical issues. Requesting emergency landing."

Sarah tensed. "Do we have clearance?"

Lou nodded. "Cleared. But they're coming in hot."

On the field, Greta and her flock were enjoying the relative peace of the feeding station. The goslings splashed in the shallow water, and the adults grazed on the fresh grass. For a moment, it felt like life had returned to normal.

But Greta's instincts prickled. She paused mid-bite, her sharp eyes scanning the horizon. The distant hum of an approaching plane grew louder, faster than usual. She honked sharply, rallying the flock.

“Get back! Move to the edge of the field!” she commanded, her voice cutting through the calm.

The geese responded immediately, flapping and waddling to safety as the noise grew deafening. Greta held her ground, watching as the metal bird roared closer. Something was wrong—it was flying too low, its path uneven.

The plane streaked overhead, its shadow sweeping across the field. Greta’s heart pounded as it descended rapidly toward the runway. She braced for impact.

In the tower, Sarah watched the scene unfold, her hands clenched into fists. The plane hit the runway with a screech of rubber and metal, skidding dangerously close to the grass. Sparks flew as the landing gear struggled to hold, and for a terrifying moment, it looked like it might veer off completely.

“Emergency crews are on their way,” Lou reported, his voice tight. “It’s holding, but barely.”

Sarah’s eyes flicked to the geese. They were huddled at the edge of the field, safe for now but visibly shaken. Greta stood at the forefront, her gaze fixed on the chaos as if daring the machine to challenge her.

The plane finally came to a halt, smoke billowing from its wheels. The emergency crews descended quickly, surrounding the aircraft and assessing the situation. The passengers were evacuated without injury, but the tension in the air was palpable.

Roger Timmons stormed into the tower minutes later, his face red with anger. “That’s it! I’m done playing nice with these birds. Do you see how close they were? One more step, and we’d be cleaning feathers off the runway!”

Sarah met his gaze, her voice calm but firm. “The geese weren’t the problem. The plane had mechanical issues. This could have happened anywhere.”

Roger wasn't convinced. "Doesn't matter. If those birds keep hovering near the runway, it's only a matter of time before we have a real disaster."

Tom entered, carrying his ever-present notebook. "Roger, you're not giving them enough credit. The geese are staying in their zones. They've adapted better than we could've hoped."

Roger threw up his hands. "It's not enough. We need guarantees, not hope."

Back on the field, Greta called a meeting of her own. The flock gathered around her, their chatter filled with worry.

"That was too close," Horace said, his feathers still ruffled. "We can't stay here. It's only a matter of time before one of those things crashes right into us."

Greta frowned. She couldn't deny the risk, but she also knew the flock didn't have many options. Leaving the airport would mean flying blind into unknown dangers.

"We need to stay alert," she said. "The humans are trying to help, but we can't rely on them completely. If the machines come too close again, we move."

"And go where?" another goose asked. "There's nothing out there for us."

"We'll figure it out," Greta replied, though her heart ached with uncertainty. She hated not having all the answers, but as a leader, she couldn't let the flock see her doubt.

The humans were equally uncertain. At the operations center, Sarah, Tom, and Lisa debated their next steps.

"The system is working, but it's fragile," Lisa said. "If we lose the geese's trust, they'll scatter, and we'll be back to square one."

Tom nodded. "We need to reinforce the deterrents around the high-risk zones. Maybe add more reflective barriers or sound devices."

Sarah tapped her pen on the table, her mind racing. "What about integrating technology? Something that allows the geese to signal us if they feel threatened."

Lisa raised an eyebrow. "You're suggesting we teach geese to communicate with humans?"

Sarah shrugged. "Why not? They're already incredibly smart. If we can develop a simple system—something visual or auditory—they could warn us before a plane gets too close."

The room fell silent as the idea sank in. It was ambitious, but not impossible.

Greta, meanwhile, was developing her own system. She began organizing the flock into smaller groups, each responsible for scouting a specific area. The scouts reported back regularly, providing updates on any changes in the humans' behavior or the movements of the machines.

"Knowledge is power," Greta told Max, who had taken on the role of her assistant. "The more we understand them, the safer we'll be."

Max nodded eagerly, his enthusiasm unshaken by the recent events. "Do you think the humans will keep helping us?"

Greta glanced toward the tower, where the humans were bustling about. "I think they're trying. But we can't wait for them to figure it out. We have to protect ourselves."

The next week brought a breakthrough. Sarah's team developed a prototype for a light-based signaling system that could be used to warn the geese of approaching planes. The system relied on simple patterns of flashing lights—green for safe, red for danger—that the geese could learn to recognize.

Tom tested the system with a small group of geese, using food rewards to reinforce the signals. To everyone's surprise, the geese picked it up quickly. Greta, ever observant, watched the process from a distance, her mind racing with possibilities.

As the humans and geese adapted to the new system, the tension at Skylark Airport began to ease. The close calls became less frequent, and the sanctuary project neared completion. For the first time in months, it felt like a true partnership was forming.

Chapter 11: A United Effort

The atmosphere at Skylark Airport buzzed with an unusual mix of urgency and optimism. For months, humans and geese had danced on the edge of conflict, but now, for the first time, there was real hope for a collaborative future. Both sides, driven by necessity and determination, began working toward a common goal: sharing the sky.

Sarah Skylark paced the operations center, her mind juggling a dozen tasks at once. In one corner, Lisa Patel was on a conference call with a local conservation group, negotiating additional funding for the sanctuary project. Across the room, Tom was hunched over a laptop, analyzing data from the new light-based signaling system that had been installed the week prior.

"Progress?" Sarah asked as she approached Tom's desk, her voice betraying both exhaustion and curiosity.

Tom looked up, his eyes bright with excitement. "Better than we expected. The geese are responding to the signals almost perfectly. We've reduced runway intrusions by 80% this week."

"That's incredible," Sarah said, allowing herself a rare smile. "If we can keep this up, we might just pull it off."

"Pulling it off" was a tall order. The challenges of maintaining safety, protecting the geese, and coordinating flights were still immense, but the system was working better than anyone had dared to hope. The next step, Sarah knew, was expanding the effort beyond Skylark Airport.

Down on the field, Greta and her flock had adapted quickly to the changes. The light signals had become part of their daily routine, and the designated feeding zones now felt like home. Even Horace, who had been the most skeptical of the humans' intentions, grudgingly admitted that things were improving.

"I'll say this much," he muttered one evening as he pecked at a patch of fresh grass. "At least they're not chasing us anymore."

Max, ever eager, turned to Greta with a grin. "Do you think it means they trust us now?"

Greta tilted her head, her sharp eyes scanning the horizon. The humans had indeed changed their approach, but trust was a tricky thing. She couldn't afford to let her guard down entirely.

"They're learning," Greta said carefully. "But trust takes time. For now, we keep doing our part and watching their every move."

Max nodded solemnly, his youthful enthusiasm tempered by Greta's steady caution. The flock, inspired by Greta's leadership, continued to adapt and thrive in their unusual home.

At the sanctuary site, the transformation was nothing short of miraculous. What had once been an abandoned quarry was now a lush wetland, teeming with native plants and shimmering pools of water. Volunteers worked tirelessly, planting reeds, building nesting platforms, and ensuring the space was ready for its future inhabitants.

Lisa stood at the edge of the largest pond, watching as a group of ducks splashed happily in the water. She turned to one of the volunteers, a young woman named Maria, who was unloading crates of aquatic plants.

"Do you think the geese will take to it?" Lisa asked, shading her eyes against the afternoon sun.

Maria smiled. "If I were a goose, I'd move in tomorrow. This place is perfect."

Lisa nodded, her heart swelling with pride and relief. The sanctuary wasn't just a solution for Skylark Airport; it was a symbol of what could be achieved when humans worked in harmony with nature. The final step would be convincing the geese to relocate—and that, Lisa knew, was easier said than done.

Back at the airport, Sarah and her team prepared for a critical meeting with the airport board. The success of the light signaling system and the progress on the sanctuary had bolstered their case, but there were still skeptics who needed convincing.

As the board members filed into the conference room, Sarah took a deep breath and began her presentation. She outlined the improvements in safety metrics, showed before-and-after photos of the sanctuary, and shared testimonials from pilots who had noticed a significant reduction in bird activity near the runways.

"This isn't just about Skylark Airport," Sarah concluded. "It's about setting a precedent for how we handle human-wildlife interactions in aviation. By working with the geese instead of against them, we've proven that coexistence is not only possible—it's effective."

The room was silent for a moment before Roger Timmons, who had been one of the plan's most vocal critics, cleared his throat.

"I'll admit, I had my doubts," Roger said, his tone grudging. "But the numbers speak for themselves. If this system keeps working, it could change the way airports operate worldwide."

Sarah allowed herself a small smile. "That's the goal."

For Greta, the humans' continued efforts were both perplexing and reassuring. She had noticed the changes at the sanctuary site, though she hadn't yet visited it herself. The flock relied on her leadership, and she wasn't about to lead them into unfamiliar territory without a thorough investigation.

One crisp morning, Greta decided it was time to see the sanctuary for herself. She selected a small group of scouts, including Max and Horace, and led them on the short flight to the site.

What they found took Greta's breath away. The sanctuary was everything the flock had been searching for: wide open spaces, plentiful food, and calm, clear water. It felt too good to be true.

"This can't be real," Horace said, his voice tinged with both awe and suspicion. "What's the catch?"

Greta didn't respond immediately. She circled the area, inspecting every detail, her sharp eyes searching for any hidden dangers. When she found none, she landed on the edge of the largest pond, her webbed feet sinking into the cool mud.

"It's real," Greta said finally, her voice soft. "But we need to be sure it's safe."

The geese spent hours exploring the sanctuary, testing its boundaries and observing the humans who worked there. Greta was impressed by their efforts, but she remained cautious. The sanctuary was a gift, but it came with risks. If the flock decided to move, they would be leaving behind the relative security of Skylark Airport for an unknown future.

When Greta and the scouts returned to the flock, she called a meeting to share what they had seen. The geese listened intently as Greta described the sanctuary, their murmurs filled with a mix of excitement and apprehension.

"It sounds perfect," Max said, his eyes shining. "Why don't we move there right now?"

Greta raised a wing to silence him. "It is perfect, Max. But we can't make this decision lightly. Moving the flock is a risk, and we need to be sure it's the right one."

The flock debated late into the night, their voices rising and falling like waves. Greta listened carefully to every concern and suggestion, weighing the options in her mind.

At Skylark Airport, Sarah and her team were preparing for the next phase of their plan: introducing the geese to the sanctuary in a way that would encourage them to stay. They set up feeding stations and shelters, carefully designed to mimic the geese's natural habitat.

Tom, who had grown particularly fond of the flock, approached Sarah with a question that had been nagging at him.

"Do you think they'll go willingly?" he asked, his voice tinged with doubt.

Sarah thought for a moment before replying. "I think they'll go if they feel safe. Greta's smart—smarter than we've given her credit for. If she sees the sanctuary as a better option, she'll lead them there."

As the days passed, the tension between humans and geese gave way to collaboration. Both sides worked tirelessly to ensure the transition was as smooth as possible. The humans refined their systems, while the geese adapted to the changes with remarkable resilience.

The sky, once a source of conflict, was becoming a shared space—a symbol of what could be achieved when two worlds worked together.

Chapter 12: Greta's Decision

The sun rose over Skylark Airport, casting a golden glow across the field where Greta's flock rested. For weeks, they had navigated the delicate balance of coexistence with the humans, learning their signals, adapting to their routines, and avoiding their machines. But now, a monumental choice loomed before them, one that would change the flock's future forever.

Greta stood apart from the others, her sharp eyes scanning the horizon. The memory of the sanctuary lingered in her mind—a haven of still water and lush greenery that seemed too perfect to be real. The scouts who had accompanied her had returned with glowing reports, but Greta's heart was heavy with doubt. Could she truly lead her flock away from the only home they had known for months? Could she trust the humans' intentions?

Max approached her, his youthful energy undimmed by the weight of the situation. "Greta, have you decided yet? Are we going to the sanctuary?"

Greta sighed, her feathers ruffling in the cool morning breeze. "It's not that simple, Max. Moving the flock is a risk. We'd be leaving behind the systems we've worked so hard to adapt to. What if the sanctuary isn't as safe as it seems?"

Max tilted his head. "But it's better than staying here, isn't it? The humans have been good to us lately. Maybe they really do want to help."

Greta admired his optimism, though it made her heart ache. She wished she could see the world as simply as Max did, but as the leader of the flock, she couldn't afford to be naïve. Every decision she made carried the weight of their survival.

"I need more time to think," Greta said finally. "This isn't a decision I can make alone."

At the operations center, Sarah Skylark sat with Tom and Lisa, reviewing the final preparations for the sanctuary. The wetland was nearly complete, with food stations, nesting areas, and deterrents to keep predators away. Everything was ready—but the geese hadn't made their move.

"They're hesitating," Tom said, tapping his pen against the edge of his notebook. "Greta doesn't trust us yet."

Sarah nodded, her gaze fixed on the map of the sanctuary. "She's smart. She knows the risks of relocating the flock. If we want her to feel safe, we need to show her that we're committed to their well-being."

Lisa leaned forward, her brow furrowed. "What if we give them a trial run? Encourage the flock to visit the sanctuary during the day and return to the airport at night. That way, they can explore it on their terms."

Tom considered the idea, nodding slowly. "It could work. We'd need to set up clear paths to guide them and monitor their movements closely."

Sarah's face lit up with a rare smile. "Let's do it. If Greta sees that the sanctuary is safe, she might just lead the flock there permanently."

That afternoon, the humans implemented their plan. Using carefully placed feeding stations and subtle visual cues, they created a pathway from the airport to the sanctuary. Tom and his team watched from a distance as the geese began to notice the changes.

Greta was the first to investigate. She approached the new feeding station cautiously, her sharp eyes scanning for any sign of danger. When she found none, she signaled to the flock, and they followed her lead.

"It's another trap," Horace muttered as he pecked at the birdseed.

"It's not a trap," Max replied, his voice filled with excitement. "They're showing us the way to the sanctuary!"

Greta remained silent, her mind racing. The humans' intentions seemed genuine, but she couldn't ignore the risks. If the flock moved to the sanctuary and something went wrong, it would be on her.

Over the next few days, the geese began exploring the pathway to the sanctuary. Greta led the flock cautiously, stopping frequently to assess their surroundings. The sanctuary was as beautiful as she remembered, its calm waters reflecting the clear blue sky. The goslings splashed happily in the ponds, while the adults grazed on the abundant vegetation.

For the first time in months, the flock seemed truly at peace. But Greta's mind was still restless. The sanctuary was perfect, but it was also unfamiliar. Could she truly trust the humans to keep it safe?

One evening, as the sun dipped below the horizon, Sarah stood on the edge of the sanctuary, watching the geese explore. Her heart swelled with a mix of pride and apprehension. They were so close to success, but she knew that Greta's trust was the final hurdle.

"She's holding back," Tom said, joining Sarah by the water's edge. "She wants to trust us, but she's not there yet."

Sarah nodded. "We need to give her a sign. Something that shows her we're committed to this partnership."

Tom frowned. "Like what?"

Sarah thought for a moment, then smiled. "Let's make the sanctuary even better. Add more food sources, build additional shelters, and create a protected area where the flock can rest undisturbed. If Greta sees that we're going above and beyond, she might finally make her decision."

The next morning, the humans began enhancing the sanctuary. Volunteers planted more reeds and grasses, built additional nesting platforms, and even installed a small fountain to keep the water circulating. The work was grueling, but the results were worth it. By the end of the day, the sanctuary was more inviting than ever.

Greta noticed the changes immediately. As she led the flock into the sanctuary that evening, she paused to examine the new additions. The humans had clearly put a lot of effort into making the space safe and welcoming. It was a gesture that didn't go unnoticed.

"They're really trying," Max said, his voice filled with awe. "Maybe we should give them a chance."

Greta looked at the young goose, her heart heavy with responsibility. Max's enthusiasm was infectious, but the decision weighed heavily on her. If she led the flock to the sanctuary permanently, there would be no turning back.

That night, Greta gathered the flock for a meeting. The geese huddled together in a circle, their murmurs filled with anticipation.

"I've made my decision," Greta began, her voice steady. "The sanctuary is safe. The humans have shown us that they're willing to work with us, not against us. It's time for us to move."

The flock erupted in cheers, their honks echoing across the field. Even Horace, who had been the most skeptical, nodded in agreement.

"It's a risk," Greta continued, "but it's one we have to take. This is our chance for a better future."

Max beamed with pride, his young heart swelling with hope. "You're the best leader we could ever ask for, Greta."

Greta smiled, though her heart was heavy with the weight of her decision. Leading the flock to the sanctuary was a leap of faith, but it was one she was willing to take.

As the geese prepared for their journey, Sarah and her team watched from a distance, their hearts filled with anticipation. The moment Greta led the flock into the sanctuary for the first time felt like a triumph—a testament to what could be achieved through trust, collaboration, and perseverance.

The sky above Skylark Airport was peaceful that evening, its vast expanse a symbol of the unity that had been achieved. For Greta and her flock, the sanctuary was more than a new home—it was a new beginning.

Chapter 13: The Storm

The sanctuary basked in a golden glow as the geese settled into their new home. Greta stood on a small rise overlooking the largest pond, her keen eyes watching the flock as they explored their surroundings. For the first time in months, she felt the tension in her chest begin to ease. The move to the sanctuary had been a leap of faith, but so far, it seemed to be paying off.

Max paddled up to her, his small wings splashing in the cool water. "It's amazing here, Greta," he said, his voice brimming with excitement. "I think we've finally found the perfect place."

Greta allowed herself a small smile. "It is amazing," she admitted. "But we can't let our guard down. There's always a challenge waiting around the corner."

Max frowned, tilting his head. "What kind of challenge?"

As if in answer, the wind picked up, rustling the reeds and sending a chill through the air. Greta's smile faded. The sanctuary might have been perfect, but nature was unpredictable. She had learned long ago that peace was often fleeting.

At Skylark Airport, Sarah Skylark was reviewing the latest reports from the sanctuary. Tom and Lisa had been monitoring the geese closely, and the data was promising. The flock had adapted quickly to their new environment, and there hadn't been a single runway intrusion since their relocation.

"It's working," Lisa said, her voice tinged with relief. "The geese are thriving, and the airport is running smoother than ever."

Sarah nodded, though a nagging feeling in the back of her mind kept her from fully relaxing. "It's working now," she said. "But we can't assume the job is done. We need to be ready for anything."

Tom glanced out the window, his brow furrowing. "Speaking of being ready for anything... have you seen the forecast? There's a storm system moving in. Could get rough over the next few days."

Sarah's stomach tightened. A storm could disrupt everything—the sanctuary, the geese, even the delicate trust they had built. "How bad are we talking?"

Tom pulled up the weather radar on his tablet, showing a swirling mass of clouds headed their way. "Severe thunderstorms, strong winds, maybe even hail. It's not going to be pretty."

The first signs of the storm appeared that evening. Dark clouds gathered on the horizon, and the air grew heavy with humidity. The geese sensed the change long before the first raindrops fell. Greta rallied the flock, her sharp honks cutting through the rising wind.

"Everyone, gather close!" she called. "We need to stay together and find shelter."

The flock huddled near the dense reeds at the edge of the largest pond, their murmurs filled with worry. Max pressed close to Greta, his eyes wide with fear.

"Will we be okay?" he asked, his voice trembling.

Greta placed a reassuring wing on his shoulder. "We'll be fine," she said, though her own heart was pounding. "We've faced worse storms before."

But as the first flash of lightning illuminated the sanctuary, Greta couldn't shake the feeling that this storm would test them in ways they had never been tested before.

At the operations center, Sarah and her team watched the storm roll in with growing unease. The radar showed a rapidly intensifying system, its path aimed directly at the sanctuary.

"We need to act fast," Sarah said, her voice steady despite the tension in the room. "If the storm hits the sanctuary too hard, the geese could panic. We can't let them scatter."

Tom nodded. "I'll head to the sanctuary and set up additional shelters. We've got some portable windbreaks in storage—I'll bring those too."

“I’m coming with you,” Sarah said, grabbing her jacket. “If things get bad, we’ll need all hands on deck.”

The storm hit with a fury that surpassed even Greta’s worst fears. The wind howled through the sanctuary, bending the reeds and churning the water into frothy waves. Rain lashed against the geese as they huddled together, their feathers soaked and their bodies trembling.

“Stay low!” Greta shouted, her voice barely audible over the roar of the storm. “Don’t move unless I tell you!”

Max pressed against her side, his small frame shivering. “It’s so loud,” he whispered, his voice barely a squeak. “What if the water rises?”

Greta’s heart ached for the young goose, but she forced herself to stay calm. “We’ll find higher ground if we need to,” she said. “But for now, we hold steady.”

Sarah and Tom arrived at the sanctuary as the storm reached its peak. The rain was relentless, soaking them to the bone as they worked to secure the shelters and reinforce the windbreaks.

“This isn’t going to hold for long,” Tom shouted over the wind, his hands gripping a tarp that threatened to tear free. “We need to check on the geese!”

Sarah nodded, her flashlight cutting through the darkness as she scanned the area. The sanctuary, which had been so serene just hours ago, was now a chaotic mess of swirling water and debris.

“There!” Sarah shouted, pointing toward the largest pond. The geese were huddled together, their silhouettes barely visible through the sheets of rain.

Greta saw the humans before the rest of the flock did. Her first instinct was to warn the others, but something about the way the humans moved stopped her. They weren’t a threat—they were trying to help.

“Stay here,” Greta told Max. “I’m going to see what they’re doing.”

Max's eyes widened. "Be careful!"

Greta nodded and stepped forward, her movements cautious but deliberate. She honked loudly, drawing the humans' attention. Sarah froze for a moment, her flashlight catching Greta's determined gaze.

"Commander Goose," Sarah murmured, a flicker of a smile crossing her face despite the chaos. "You're still keeping things under control, I see."

She turned to Tom. "Let's guide them to the higher ground near the windbreaks. It's their best chance."

With Greta's help, Sarah and Tom guided the flock to the sheltered area. It was a slow and arduous process, the wind and rain fighting them every step of the way. But Greta's leadership and the humans' determination carried them through.

By the time the flock reached the windbreaks, the storm's intensity had begun to wane. The geese huddled together, their exhaustion evident but their spirits unbroken.

Chapter 14: Lessons from the Flock

The storm had left the sanctuary and Skylark Airport scarred but not defeated. Broken reeds lay flattened across the ponds, mud trails wove through the once-pristine grass, and the geese, though shaken, had emerged stronger for their ordeal.

Greta stood at the water's edge as the morning sun kissed the landscape, her sharp eyes taking in the quiet resilience of her flock. She knew that they had survived more than a storm—they had proven to themselves, and perhaps even to the humans, that they could adapt and thrive no matter the odds.

Max bounded up to her, his energy undeterred by the previous night's chaos. "Greta! Did you see how everyone worked together? Even Horace was helping with the goslings!"

Greta turned, her gaze softening as she watched the younger geese splash tentatively in the pond. "It was a good reminder, Max. We're stronger when we stand together."

"But the humans helped too," Max said, his eyes wide with wonder. "They didn't have to, but they stayed out in the storm for us."

Greta didn't respond immediately. The humans' actions during the storm had surprised her, their efforts revealing a side of them she hadn't expected. She had always been cautious, even mistrustful, but the storm had shown her that perhaps there was more to these creatures than she had assumed.

At the operations center, Sarah Skylark stood with Tom and Lisa, their clothes still damp from the storm. The exhaustion in the room was palpable, but so was the quiet pride.

"We made it through," Tom said, pouring himself a much-needed cup of coffee. "The geese are safe, and the sanctuary held up better than I expected."

Lisa nodded, scrolling through the photos she had taken during the storm. "It's incredible how resilient they are. Greta especially. She kept that flock together through the worst of it."

Sarah leaned against the table, her mind replaying the moment when she had locked eyes with Greta during the storm. There had been something in the goose's gaze—a spark of understanding, maybe even trust.

"They're teaching us as much as we're helping them," Sarah said thoughtfully. "We've spent months trying to control them, but maybe the real lesson here is how to adapt alongside them."

Tom raised an eyebrow. "Are you saying we should start taking lessons from the geese?"

"Why not?" Sarah said with a faint smile. "They've figured out how to live in harmony with their environment. Maybe it's time we did the same."

Greta had similar thoughts as she led the flock through their morning routine. The sanctuary had become a place of healing, but it was also a place of learning. The geese were rediscovering old habits while forging new ones, adapting to their surroundings with the same determination that had carried them through the storm.

Horace, who had once been the loudest critic of the humans, now seemed quieter, more reflective. As he approached Greta, his usual gruffness was replaced with a tone of respect.

"I'll admit, Greta," he said, "I didn't think this sanctuary idea would work. But last night... well, the humans proved me wrong."

Greta tilted her head, surprised but pleased by Horace's admission. "They did more than I expected too. But we can't forget that we've earned this place. We worked for it just as hard as they did."

Horace nodded. "You're right. We didn't just survive—we thrived."

As the days passed, the humans and geese settled into a new rhythm. Sarah and her team continued to refine the systems at the sanctuary, using data from the storm to improve the shelters and expand the feeding zones. Meanwhile, the geese adapted to their new home with a combination of instinct and learned behavior, their bond with the humans growing stronger with each passing day.

One afternoon, Tom invited Sarah to join him for an observation session at the sanctuary. Armed with binoculars and notebooks, they sat on a small hill overlooking the largest pond.

"Watch Greta," Tom said, pointing to the goose who stood at the center of the flock. "She's always the first to investigate new things, but she's careful. She never acts without considering the safety of the others."

Sarah adjusted her binoculars, focusing on Greta as she led a group of goslings to the edge of the pond. The older goose paused, scanning the area with sharp eyes before signaling the others to follow.

"She's remarkable," Sarah said. "A true leader."

Tom nodded. "There's a lot we can learn from her. She's adaptable, decisive, and protective. She trusts her instincts but also knows when to lean on the strength of the group."

Sarah smiled. "It's funny, isn't it? We came into this thinking we had all the answers, but it turns out the geese had more to teach us than we realized."

Greta, unaware of the humans' admiration, was focused on a new challenge: teaching the younger geese the skills they would need to thrive. She spent hours showing them how to forage for food, avoid potential dangers, and navigate the sanctuary's various zones.

Max was her most eager student, always the first to volunteer and the last to give up. "What's next, Greta?" he asked one morning, his eyes shining with excitement. "Are you going to teach us how to fly in formation?"

Greta chuckled, her feathers ruffling in amusement. "One step at a time, Max. Formation flying is important, but it's also about teamwork. You can't lead if you don't know how to follow."

Max tilted his head, considering her words. "So it's like how you listen to the humans sometimes? Even though you're in charge?"

Greta paused, surprised by Max's insight. "Exactly," she said. "Leadership isn't just about giving orders. It's about knowing when to listen and when to act."

At the sanctuary, the bond between humans and geese continued to grow. Sarah spent more time observing the flock, her respect for their intelligence and resilience deepening with each encounter. She began to notice patterns in their behavior—how they communicated with subtle honks and gestures, how they worked together to solve problems, and how they always put the needs of the group above their own.

One day, as she watched Greta lead the flock through a particularly tricky patch of mud, Sarah turned to Tom with a grin. "I think Greta might be a better manager than me."

Tom laughed. "Don't let Roger hear you say that. He might start asking for leadership workshops from Commander Goose."

The geese, too, were learning from the humans. Greta had grown accustomed to their presence, even seeking out Sarah or Tom when she sensed a problem. It wasn't trust, exactly, but it was something close—a mutual understanding born of shared experience.

Chapter 15: Bridging the Gap

The sanctuary at Skylark Airport had become more than just a refuge; it was now a place where two vastly different worlds intersected in harmony. The once-impossible task of humans and geese coexisting had turned into a delicate, ongoing collaboration. But the work was far from over, and the challenges of fully bridging the gap between these worlds remained as daunting as ever.

Greta stood on the shore of the sanctuary's largest pond, the cool morning breeze ruffling her feathers. Her flock had settled into a steady routine, and for the first time in months, a sense of calm permeated their days. But Greta's sharp mind was never at rest. She watched as a group of younger geese practiced taking off and landing, their movements clumsy but full of enthusiasm.

Max was among them, his boundless energy making up for his lack of skill. He flapped his wings furiously, managing a wobbly liftoff before splashing back into the water with a loud squawk.

"You almost had it," Greta said as Max paddled toward her, his eyes wide with determination.

"Almost isn't good enough," Max replied, shaking water from his feathers. "I want to be ready when it's time to fly with the flock."

Greta nodded, her gaze drifting toward the horizon. The sanctuary was safe for now, but she knew their journey wasn't over. Migrating to new lands would be their ultimate test, and every member of the flock needed to be prepared.

At the operations center, Sarah Skylark sat with Tom and Lisa, reviewing their progress. The sanctuary was thriving, and reports from pilots indicated that bird-related incidents had dropped to near zero. Still, Sarah couldn't shake the feeling that there was more to be done.

"We've built the sanctuary, but we haven't solved the larger problem," Sarah said, tapping her pen against the table. "The geese are here because their natural habitats are disappearing. If we don't address that, we're just putting a band-aid on the situation."

Lisa nodded. "You're right. Skylark is a success story, but it's not scalable. Other airports, other species—they all face similar challenges."

Tom leaned back in his chair, his brow furrowed in thought. "Maybe the answer lies in education. If we can show people what we've done here, they might be inspired to replicate it elsewhere."

Sarah considered this, her mind racing. "We need a way to share what we've learned—not just with other airports, but with everyone. If we can change how people think about wildlife, we might actually make a lasting impact."

The opportunity to bridge the gap came unexpectedly. A group of journalists had heard about the sanctuary's success and reached out for a tour. Sarah hesitated at first, knowing the media could be both an ally and a distraction. But Lisa convinced her it was worth the risk.

"We need to tell this story," Lisa said. "The more people know about what we've achieved, the more support we'll get."

On the day of the tour, Sarah and Tom greeted a small group of reporters at the sanctuary's entrance. The journalists were skeptical at first, their questions laced with doubt.

"So you're telling me geese and airplanes can coexist?" one reporter asked, raising an eyebrow.

"They already are," Sarah replied, leading the group toward the pond. "But it's not just about coexistence. It's about finding solutions that work for everyone."

As they walked, the reporters marveled at the sanctuary's design. They saw feeding stations, nesting platforms, and the carefully maintained pathways that allowed the geese to move freely without interfering with airport operations. But what impressed them most was the flock itself.

Greta, ever the leader, watched the humans from a distance. She didn't trust them completely, but she had learned to tolerate their presence. When Sarah approached the pond, Greta stepped forward, her sharp eyes meeting Sarah's.

"This is Greta," Sarah said, gesturing to the goose. "She's the reason this works. Her leadership keeps the flock organized and safe."

The reporters snapped photos, their skepticism giving way to admiration. One journalist leaned closer to Sarah and whispered, "Is it just me, or does she look like she's in charge?"

Sarah smiled. "She is."

The media coverage of the sanctuary sparked a wave of interest. Articles, videos, and social media posts spread the story of Skylark Airport's innovative approach to wildlife management. Conservation groups, airport officials, and even schoolchildren reached out, eager to learn more.

For Sarah, the response was both overwhelming and inspiring. She began receiving invitations to speak at conferences and participate in workshops. At each event, she shared the lessons she had learned from working with the geese, emphasizing the importance of collaboration and adaptability.

"Wildlife isn't the problem," Sarah said during one presentation. "It's how we respond to it. When we treat nature as an adversary, we all lose. But when we work together, we can find solutions that benefit everyone."

Back at the sanctuary, the geese continued to adapt. Greta's leadership remained steadfast, but she began to notice a subtle change in her flock. They were becoming more independent, their confidence growing with each passing day. Even Horace, who had once been the loudest critic, had taken on a mentoring role, helping the younger geese refine their flying skills.

Max, in particular, had flourished under Greta's guidance. One afternoon, he approached her with a question that had been on his mind for weeks.

"Greta, what happens after this?" he asked, his voice hesitant. "I mean, this place is amazing, but we can't stay here forever, can we?"

Greta looked at Max, her heart swelling with pride and worry. He was right, of course. The sanctuary was a temporary haven, but their journey would continue.

"We'll know when it's time to move," Greta said gently. "But for now, we focus on becoming stronger. When the time comes, we'll be ready."

Sarah, too, was thinking about the future. The success of the sanctuary had been a turning point, but she knew it wasn't the end of the story. One evening, as she stood at the edge of the pond, she found herself watching Greta again. The goose was perched on a small rise, her silhouette framed by the setting sun.

"You're still teaching us," Sarah murmured. "Even when we think we've figured it all out, you show us there's more to learn."

Tom joined her, his hands stuffed into his jacket pockets. "She's remarkable, isn't she? I've worked with animals my whole life, but I've never seen anything like her."

Sarah nodded. "She's not just a leader for her flock. She's a leader for us too."

As the weeks passed, the bond between humans and geese deepened. The sanctuary became a place of learning and collaboration, a living example of what could be achieved when two worlds worked together. For Greta and her flock, it was a chance to thrive. For Sarah and her team, it was a chance to make a difference.

But the journey wasn't over. The gap between humans and wildlife was vast, and bridging it would take more than one sanctuary. It would take a global effort, driven by the lessons learned at Skylark Airport.

Chapter 16: A Collaborative Flight

The air was crisp and calm, the kind of morning that hinted at a change on the horizon. At the sanctuary, Greta stood on the hill overlooking the largest pond, her sharp eyes scanning the open sky. Something about the day felt different—charged with energy. The flock had been thriving for weeks, their routines seamless, their confidence growing. But Greta knew that comfort could make them complacent, and a leader's duty was to prepare for what came next.

Max flapped up beside her, his wings stronger and steadier than ever. "Greta," he said breathlessly, "Horace has been teaching us new formations! You should see how well we're doing."

Greta glanced at him, a flicker of pride in her gaze. "Good," she said. "We'll need those formations when it's time to leave."

Max's enthusiasm faltered. "Leave? But why? The sanctuary is perfect."

"It is," Greta agreed. "But migration isn't just about finding a place to rest. It's about moving forward, finding new opportunities. This sanctuary has been a gift, but we can't stay here forever."

Max nodded, though his young mind struggled to grasp the enormity of her words. "Do you think the humans will help us when it's time to go?"

Greta looked toward the humans' observation post, where Sarah and Tom were setting up equipment. "I think they've shown they're willing to try. But we'll need to lead the way."

At the observation post, Sarah Skylark sipped her coffee, her eyes fixed on the geese below. The sanctuary was running smoothly, but like Greta, Sarah was always thinking ahead. She had started receiving reports of other migratory birds passing through the region, a sign that the season was changing. The geese would need to migrate soon, and Sarah wanted to ensure their journey was as safe as possible.

Tom joined her, carrying a stack of notes. "I've been monitoring their flight patterns," he said, setting the papers down. "Greta's been organizing practice runs with the flock. It's impressive—they're more coordinated than some human teams I've worked with."

Sarah smiled. "She's a better leader than most humans I know."

Tom chuckled. "True. But migration is a whole different challenge. They'll need clear skies, minimal interference, and safe stopping points along the way."

Sarah's smile faded. "And that's where it gets tricky. We can't control what happens once they leave the sanctuary."

"Maybe not," Tom said, "but we can give them the best possible start. I've been working on a plan to guide them through their first leg. It involves temporary no-fly zones and an escort team to ensure they stay clear of air traffic."

Sarah raised an eyebrow. "An escort team? Are you suggesting we fly with them?"

"Not us," Tom said, grinning. "Drones."

The idea of drones assisting the geese was met with a mix of excitement and skepticism at Skylark Airport. Roger Timmons, ever the curmudgeon, voiced his concerns loudly during a team meeting.

"Drones? Really?" he said, crossing his arms. "What happens when one of those things malfunctions and ends up scaring the geese instead of helping them?"

Tom held his ground. "The drones are equipped with GPS and obstacle-avoidance systems. They'll stay at a safe distance, just visible enough for the geese to follow. It's about providing guidance, not interference."

Sarah chimed in. "We've already proven that technology and wildlife can coexist. This is just an extension of that. If it gives the geese a better chance of making their migration safely, it's worth trying."

After much debate, the plan was approved. A team of engineers worked tirelessly to modify the drones, ensuring they were quiet, efficient, and capable of maintaining a steady pace alongside the flock.

On the morning of the first trial flight, excitement buzzed through the sanctuary. The geese sensed that something significant was happening. Greta gathered the flock, her honks commanding their attention.

"Today, we test our strength," she said. "We've worked hard to prepare for this moment. Stick to your formations, follow the signals, and trust one another. We are a team, and together, we can conquer the skies."

Max's chest puffed with pride as he took his place near Greta. The older geese, including Horace, nodded solemnly, their determination clear.

The humans watched anxiously as the trial began. Two drones hovered just above the trees, their movements smooth and deliberate. Greta honked sharply, signaling the flock to take off. With a flurry of wings, they rose into the air, their formations tight and coordinated.

"Look at that," Tom said, his voice filled with awe. "They're following the drones perfectly."

Sarah couldn't help but smile. "Greta's leading them, as always. The drones are just a backup."

The flock flew a designated loop around the sanctuary, the drones guiding them through subtle changes in altitude and direction. The younger geese struggled at first, but under Greta's watchful eye, they quickly found their rhythm.

When the flock returned to the sanctuary, the humans erupted into cheers. Greta landed gracefully, her flock close behind. Max was practically glowing with excitement.

"Did you see that, Greta?" he exclaimed. "We did it!"

Greta nodded, her feathers ruffling in satisfaction. "You all did well. But this was just the beginning."

Over the next few weeks, the geese and humans worked together to refine the migration plan. The drones were programmed with precise routes, and temporary no-fly zones were coordinated with nearby airports to ensure the flock's safety. Sarah and Tom even reached out to local wildlife organizations, arranging for safe stopping points along the migration path.

For Greta, the preparations were both exciting and bittersweet. She had grown to appreciate the sanctuary and the humans who had made it possible, but she knew that her duty was to lead the flock forward.

On the morning of the migration, the sanctuary was filled with a sense of anticipation. The geese gathered on the hill, their wings ready, their spirits high. Greta stood at the forefront, her heart pounding with both pride and apprehension.

Sarah and Tom watched from the observation post, their emotions mirroring Greta's. The drones were in position, the sky was clear, and the flock was ready.

"It's time," Sarah said softly.

Greta honked sharply, signaling the flock to take off. With a thunderous roar of wings, they rose into the air, their formations as perfect as Greta had trained them to be. The drones hovered above, guiding them toward the horizon.

As the flock disappeared into the distance, Sarah felt a pang of both loss and hope. "Do you think they'll make it?" she asked.

Tom nodded. "If Greta's leading them? Absolutely."

For Greta, the flight was a test of everything they had learned. The drones provided guidance, but it was her leadership that kept the flock steady and focused. As they soared through the sky, Greta felt a surge of pride. They were not just surviving—they were thriving.

Chapter 17: The First Migration

The dawn broke over the countryside in a symphony of colors, painting the horizon with streaks of gold and pink. Greta perched on a small rise, her sharp eyes scanning the landscape as the flock stirred behind her. This was the day they had been preparing for—their first full migration as a unified flock. The sanctuary had been a safe haven, but instinct and necessity pushed them forward. Greta knew that leading the flock on this journey would test everything they had learned.

Max was the first to approach her, his youthful energy barely contained. "Greta! Are we really doing it today? The big flight?"

Greta nodded, her feathers ruffling in the gentle breeze. "Yes, Max. The weather is clear, and the humans have set up everything we need. It's time."

Max's face lit up with a mix of excitement and nervousness. "I've been practicing so much! I'm ready."

Greta smiled softly. "I know you are. But remember, this isn't just about flying. It's about working together, staying focused, and trusting the flock."

Behind them, Horace let out a loud honk. "Let's get moving, then! We've been cooped up here long enough."

At Skylark Airport, Sarah Skylark stood with Tom and Lisa, their attention focused on the drones' control interface. The flight path had been meticulously planned, taking into account weather conditions, air traffic, and natural stopping points for the geese to rest and refuel.

"This is it," Sarah said, her voice a mix of anticipation and anxiety. "If they make it through this migration, it'll prove that coexistence is possible."

Tom adjusted his headset, his eyes scanning the live feed from the drones. "They've got everything they need: a clear path, safe zones, and Greta leading the way. If any flock can do it, it's this one."

Lisa nodded, her fingers tapping nervously on the edge of the console. "Let's just hope the weather holds."

The flock gathered in a tight formation as Greta moved to the front. She honked sharply, her signal cutting through the morning air.

"Take your positions," she commanded, her voice steady and authoritative. "We fly as one. Stay together, follow the signals, and watch out for each other."

Max found his spot near the center of the formation, his wings trembling with anticipation. Horace took a place near the rear, his experienced eyes scanning for potential stragglers.

As the flock prepared to take off, the humans watched from the observation post. Sarah raised her binoculars, her heart pounding as Greta gave the final signal. With a unified flurry of wings, the geese launched into the sky, their V-formation slicing through the crisp morning air.

The first leg of the journey was smooth, the drones hovering at a safe distance to guide the flock. Greta set a steady pace, her sharp instincts and months of training ensuring that the flock stayed coordinated. Below them, the landscape stretched out in a patchwork of fields, rivers, and forests.

Max marveled at the view, his eyes wide with wonder. "It's so beautiful up here, Greta! I've never seen anything like it."

Greta allowed herself a brief smile. "Keep your focus, Max. The journey has just begun."

The drones emitted soft pulses of light, signaling subtle course corrections. The geese responded seamlessly, their movements precise and synchronized. From the observation post, Tom watched with pride.

"They're doing it," he said, his voice filled with awe. "Look at how perfectly they're following the signals."

Sarah nodded, though her gaze remained fixed on the screen. "It's all Greta. She's keeping them steady."

As the flock approached their first rest stop—a secluded wetland designated as a safe zone—Greta honked to signal the descent. The geese landed gracefully, their wings folding as they waded into the cool water to drink and forage.

Max paddled over to Greta, his excitement uncontainable. "We're doing so well, Greta! This is easier than I thought."

Greta chuckled softly. "Don't get too comfortable, Max. We've still got a long way to go."

Horace joined them, his gruff voice tinged with respect. "You've got a good head on your shoulders, Greta. I'll admit, I wasn't sure about all this drone business, but it's working."

Greta nodded. "The humans have done their part. Now it's up to us to finish what we started."

The next leg of the journey brought its own challenges. The wind picked up, creating turbulence that tested the flock's endurance. Greta adjusted their formation, using her experience to shield the younger geese from the worst of the gusts.

"Hold steady!" she called, her voice cutting through the roar of the wind. "We've trained for this. Trust your wings."

Max struggled to keep his place, but the encouragement of the flock kept him going. Horace flew beside him, offering quiet words of support.

"You're doing fine, kid," Horace said. "Just stay in the pocket."

At the observation post, Sarah and her team monitored the flock's progress closely. The drones provided real-time data, allowing them to make adjustments to the flight path as needed.

"The wind is stronger than we expected," Lisa said, her brow furrowed. "Should we signal them to rest earlier than planned?"

Sarah shook her head. "Not yet. Greta's got them under control. Let's trust her instincts."

Tom pointed to the screen, where the drones had adjusted their positions to account for the wind. "Look at that. They're adapting in real time. This is exactly why we designed the system."

As the flock neared their second rest stop, a sudden disturbance caught Greta's attention. A flock of starlings had entered their airspace, their chaotic movements creating a potential hazard.

"Spread out!" Greta honked, her voice urgent. "Give them space!"

The geese adjusted their formation, their training evident as they avoided the starlings without losing cohesion. Greta guided them through the turbulence, her heart pounding with the effort.

When they reached the rest stop, the geese landed with a collective sigh of relief. Max collapsed onto the grass, his wings trembling.

"That was intense," he said, looking up at Greta with wide eyes. "But we made it."

Greta nodded, her chest heaving with exertion. "And we'll keep making it. One challenge at a time."

By the time the flock reached their final destination—a sprawling wetland far to the south—the sun was setting, casting a golden glow over the water. The geese landed one by one, their exhaustion tempered by a sense of triumph.

Greta stood at the edge of the pond, watching as the flock settled in. Max waddled up to her, his face beaming with pride.

"We did it, Greta," he said. "We really did it."

Greta looked out over the peaceful landscape, her heart swelling with pride and gratitude. "Yes, Max. We did."

At the observation post, Sarah and her team celebrated the flock's successful migration. The data from the drones would provide invaluable insights for future efforts, but for Sarah, the real victory was seeing the geese thrive.

"They're safe," Sarah said, her voice soft. "That's all that matters."

Tom raised a cup of coffee in a mock toast. "Here's to Greta and her incredible flock."

For Greta, the journey had been more than just a test of endurance—it had been a testament to the strength of unity and collaboration. As she looked up at the star-filled sky, she felt a deep sense of accomplishment. The migration was only the beginning, but it was proof that they could overcome any obstacle together.

Chapter 18: The New Normal

The wetlands that the flock now called home stretched as far as the eye could see, shimmering under the morning sun. Greta stood on a small hill overlooking the largest pond, her keen eyes scanning the horizon. The air was alive with the sounds of birdsong and the gentle rustle of reeds, a symphony that seemed to welcome them into this new chapter of their lives.

It had been weeks since their migration, and the geese had settled into a steady rhythm. For the first time in what felt like ages, they were free to live without fear of interference from humans or machines. But even in this haven, Greta's mind remained sharp, her instincts on high alert. The journey had taught her that peace was fragile and that vigilance was the price of survival.

Max paddled up to the hill, his small wings splashing in the clear water. "Greta! Did you see the fish in the shallow pond? They're everywhere! Horace says they're a sign that this place is really healthy."

Greta turned to him, her feathers ruffling in the breeze. "That's good news, Max. A strong ecosystem means we'll have everything we need here."

Max tilted his head. "Do you think we'll stay here forever?"

Greta hesitated, her gaze drifting back to the horizon. "Maybe," she said. "But even if we do, we need to be ready for whatever comes next. The world doesn't stay the same for long."

At Skylark Airport, Sarah Skylark was reviewing the data from the flock's migration with Tom and Lisa. The drones had performed flawlessly, and the geese's journey had been smoother than anyone had dared to hope. Yet Sarah knew their work was far from over.

"The wetlands are perfect for now," Sarah said, her pen tapping against the table. "But we can't assume they'll stay that way. Climate change, human expansion—there are so many factors we can't control."

Lisa nodded, scrolling through satellite images of the wetlands. "We need to think long-term. If this habitat becomes uninhabitable, we'll need to guide them to another one."

Tom leaned back in his chair, his expression thoughtful. "It's not just about this flock, either. What we've done here could be a blueprint for other species, other airports. We've proven that coexistence is possible."

Sarah smiled faintly. "Now we just need to make it sustainable."

For the geese, life in the wetlands was a mix of rediscovery and adaptation. The young ones, like Max, marveled at the abundance of food and the open skies, while the older geese, like Horace, took solace in the stability they had found. Greta, as always, remained the steadfast leader, her honks guiding the flock through their daily routines.

But even in this peaceful setting, challenges arose. One afternoon, as the geese were foraging near the edge of the wetland, Greta noticed a disturbance in the water. A heron had claimed the area as its own, its sharp beak darting threateningly toward the younger geese.

"Stay back!" Greta honked, rushing forward to confront the heron. The two birds faced off, their postures tense.

Horace joined her, his deep honks adding to the warning. "This is our space now," he said. "You'd best move along."

The heron hesitated, its piercing eyes scanning the geese. After a tense moment, it took to the air, its wings casting a shadow over the pond as it flew to another part of the wetland.

Max watched the scene unfold, his eyes wide. "Greta, that was amazing! You didn't even back down."

Greta turned to him, her gaze steady. "This is our home now, Max. It's up to us to protect it."

Meanwhile, Sarah and her team were working to ensure the wetlands remained a safe haven. They partnered with local conservation groups to monitor water quality, plant more vegetation, and install wildlife cameras to track the health of the ecosystem. The project had become a model for other airports, sparking a wave of interest from organizations around the world.

One day, as Sarah walked through the wetlands with a group of volunteers, she spotted Greta perched on the hill. Their eyes met briefly, and Sarah couldn't help but smile.

"She's still watching us," Sarah said to Tom, who was carrying a clipboard filled with notes. "Even here, she's making sure we're doing our part."

Tom chuckled. "She's not just a leader for the flock. She's holding us accountable too."

As the weeks turned into months, the geese and humans settled into a new normal. The wetlands thrived under the combined care of both species, a testament to what could be achieved through collaboration and respect.

For Greta, the change was profound. She had always seen humans as a threat, but their actions had begun to shift her perspective. They weren't perfect, but they had proven themselves capable of learning, adapting, and even helping.

One evening, as the flock gathered for the night, Greta stood on the hill and addressed them.

"We've come a long way," she said, her voice carrying over the still water. "We've faced challenges, but we've also found allies. This wetland is a gift, but it's also a responsibility. We must protect it, not just for ourselves but for all who share it."

Max honked enthusiastically, his youthful energy infectious. "We'll do it, Greta! Together!"

The flock echoed his sentiment, their honks filling the air with a sense of unity.

At Skylark Airport, Sarah, Tom, and Lisa prepared for their next project: expanding the sanctuary model to other regions. They held workshops, gave presentations, and worked tirelessly to share their findings with anyone willing to listen.

"This is just the beginning," Sarah said during a meeting with airport officials from another city. "What we've learned here can change the way we think about wildlife and aviation. It's not about choosing one over the other—it's about finding a balance."

The officials nodded, their interest piqued. One of them, a tall man with glasses, leaned forward. "If this works at Skylark, it can work anywhere."

Back at the wetlands, Greta watched as a new flock of migratory birds arrived, their calls filling the air. She greeted them with a series of welcoming honks, her leadership extending beyond her own flock to include the broader community of birds that shared the wetlands.

Max approached her, his eyes wide with curiosity. "Who are they, Greta?"

"They're travelers, like we were," Greta said. "And now, they're part of this place too."

Max tilted his head. "Do you think they'll stay?"

Greta considered the question, her gaze drifting to the horizon. "Maybe. Or maybe they'll move on. Either way, we'll help them while they're here."

Chapter 19: Greta's Legacy

The wetlands stretched wide under a golden sky, its ponds shimmering with reflections of the rising sun. Greta stood atop the highest hill, her silhouette outlined against the morning light. Below her, the flock stirred, their honks mingling with the hum of awakening nature. The sanctuary was thriving, and so were its inhabitants. But Greta's sharp eyes remained fixed on the horizon, a reminder that her work as a leader was never done.

Max bounded up to her side, his wings flapping with excitement. "Good morning, Greta! Did you see the sunrise? It's brighter than yesterday!"

Greta glanced at the young goose, a soft smile tugging at her beak. "Every sunrise is brighter when the flock is strong, Max."

Max puffed out his chest, his youthful enthusiasm unshaken. "We're the strongest flock ever, thanks to you!"

Greta's gaze softened as she turned to the bustling activity below. It was true—the flock was stronger than ever. Their journey, marked by challenges and victories, had transformed them into a united and resilient community. But Greta's mind lingered on the lessons she had learned, lessons she hoped would guide the flock long after her time.

At Skylark Airport, Sarah Skylark was preparing for a conference where she would present the sanctuary project's long-term impact. The data collected over the months since the geese's migration showed more than just success—it revealed the potential for a global shift in how humans approached coexistence with wildlife.

"Greta's flock proved what's possible," Sarah said during a team meeting. "But now it's up to us to take what we've learned and apply it on a larger scale."

Tom nodded, spreading out a map of regional airports. "We've already received interest from three other airports. If we can replicate the sanctuary model and adapt it to their local ecosystems, we could create a network of safe zones for migratory birds."

Lisa chimed in, her excitement evident. "And it's not just about birds. What we've done here could apply to other species—deer near highways, fish in shipping lanes. It's about rethinking how we share spaces with nature."

Sarah smiled, her pride tempered by the weight of their responsibility. "Let's make sure we do it right. This isn't just a project—it's a legacy."

Greta's legacy was already taking shape among the flock. The younger geese, inspired by her leadership, had begun taking on roles of their own. Max had become an enthusiastic teacher, showing the goslings how to forage and practice formation flying. Horace, once a skeptic, now served as a mentor, his gruff wisdom guiding the flock through challenges.

One evening, as the geese gathered for their nightly rest, Max approached Greta with a question that had been on his mind for days.

"Greta," he began hesitantly, "how did you know what to do when we first arrived at Skylark Airport? Weren't you scared?"

Greta tilted her head, her gaze thoughtful. "I was scared, Max. But fear isn't a bad thing. It keeps us alert, makes us careful. What matters is how we respond to it."

Max nodded, his eyes wide with understanding. "You responded by leading us. Does that mean I could lead someday too?"

Greta studied him for a moment, her heart swelling with pride. "Leadership isn't about being the loudest or the strongest. It's about caring for the flock and making decisions that benefit everyone. If you can do that, Max, then yes—you could lead."

Back at the wetlands, the humans and geese continued to work together in quiet harmony. Sarah and her team visited regularly, conducting surveys and ensuring the sanctuary remained a safe and thriving ecosystem. But their presence had become less about monitoring and more about learning. They observed the geese with awe, taking note of their intricate communication, their teamwork, and their unwavering commitment to one another.

One afternoon, as Sarah stood by the edge of the largest pond, she spotted Greta watching her from a nearby hill. Their eyes met briefly, a silent exchange of mutual respect.

"She's remarkable," Sarah said softly, turning to Tom. "Every time I see her, I'm reminded of how much we still have to learn."

Tom nodded, his gaze fixed on the flock. "She's not just leading them—she's setting an example for us too. Coexistence isn't about control; it's about understanding."

Greta's influence extended beyond her flock. The arrival of other migratory birds had created a bustling, interconnected community at the wetlands. Ducks, herons, and even swans now shared the space, their presence a testament to the sanctuary's success. Greta took it upon herself to welcome the newcomers, her honks carrying messages of caution and cooperation.

Max, ever curious, watched as Greta interacted with a group of swans one morning. "Greta, why do you talk to them? They're not part of our flock."

"They're part of our world," Greta replied. "The wetlands belong to all of us. The stronger our connections, the safer we'll all be."

Max tilted his head, his admiration for Greta growing with every word. "You always know what to do."

Greta chuckled softly. "Not always, Max. But I've learned to listen—to the flock, to the land, and even to the humans. That's how we find our way."

The humans, too, were learning to listen. Sarah's presentations at conferences and workshops inspired a wave of interest in wildlife-friendly design. Airports around the world began implementing similar sanctuaries, each adapted to the needs of their local ecosystems.

During one such presentation, Sarah shared a photo of Greta standing at the edge of the wetlands, her silhouette framed by the setting sun.

"This is Greta," Sarah said, her voice filled with emotion. "She's not just a goose—she's a leader, a teacher, and a symbol of what's possible when we choose to work with nature instead of against it. Her legacy is one of hope, resilience, and the belief that the sky truly is for everyone."

The audience erupted in applause, their enthusiasm a reflection of the impact Greta's story had made.

As the seasons changed, the wetlands transformed into a vibrant haven, teeming with life. Greta watched with quiet pride as her flock thrived, their bonds stronger than ever. But even as she celebrated their success, she remained mindful of the future. Her legacy wasn't just about what she had accomplished—it was about what she would leave behind.

Chapter 20: A Sky for All

Greta stood on her familiar hill, watching as her flock stirred below. It had been a year since they first arrived at Skylark Airport, their lives entangled with the humans who had initially been a source of fear and conflict. Now, as Greta gazed out over the sanctuary, she saw something she could never have imagined back then: harmony.

The wetlands had become a bustling hub of life. Greta's flock shared the space with other migratory birds, local wildlife, and even the occasional human visitor. Every honk, chirp, and rustle in the reeds spoke of a thriving ecosystem. Yet Greta's sharp eyes stayed trained on the horizon. The skies were vast, and though this corner of the world was peaceful, she knew the struggle for coexistence was far from over.

Max bounded up the hill, his wings now strong and steady after a season of growth. He stood taller, his feathers sleek and vibrant, but his youthful enthusiasm remained undiminished.

"Greta, we just finished another practice flight!" he said, his voice full of pride. "Everyone's getting better at the formations. Even Horace says so."

Greta turned to him, a soft smile on her beak. "Good work, Max. Strong formations keep us united. But remember, flying isn't just about strength—it's about precision, timing, and trust."

Max tilted his head, his expression thoughtful. "Like how we trust the humans to keep the sanctuary safe?"

Greta nodded, her gaze drifting to the observation post where Sarah and Tom were setting up equipment. "Yes. Trust goes both ways, Max. It's what makes everything possible."

At Skylark Airport, Sarah Skylark sat in the operations center with Tom and Lisa, reviewing the final preparations for a presentation that would mark the culmination of their work. The success of the sanctuary had sparked global interest, and they were now preparing to share their findings at an international conference on wildlife conservation.

"We've come a long way," Lisa said, scrolling through a slideshow of images: the wetlands teeming with life, the geese in perfect V-formation, and Greta standing tall on her hill. "But this is just the beginning."

Sarah nodded, her fingers tapping the edge of the table. "We've proven that coexistence is possible, but scaling this model will take more than goodwill. It'll take commitment, resources, and a shift in how people think about wildlife."

Tom leaned back in his chair, his expression thoughtful. "The drones were a game-changer. If we can adapt that technology for other species—bats, whales, even urban animals—we might actually change the way humans interact with nature."

Sarah smiled. "And it all started with Greta."

As the day unfolded, the wetlands became a flurry of activity. The geese honked loudly, practicing their formations and helping the younger birds prepare for their next migration. Greta moved among them, offering quiet guidance and steady leadership. She had become more than just a leader—she was a symbol of resilience and hope, not just for her flock but for the entire community.

Max approached her again, his eyes filled with curiosity. "Greta, do you ever think about what it was like before we came here? Back when we were at Skylark?"

Greta tilted her head, her gaze distant. "I think about it often, Max. It reminds me of how far we've come—and how much we've learned."

Max nodded. "Do you think the humans learned too?"

"They did," Greta said. "They learned to see us not as obstacles but as partners. And we learned to trust them, even when it wasn't easy."

At the conference, Sarah stood before a packed audience of conservationists, scientists, and policymakers. The room buzzed with anticipation as she stepped up to the podium, her voice steady and confident.

"A year ago," Sarah began, "our airport faced a challenge that many of you are familiar with: the conflict between human progress and wildlife. The skies, once shared freely by all creatures, had become battlegrounds. But through innovation, collaboration, and a willingness to adapt, we found a way to coexist."

She clicked to the next slide, which showed a photograph of Greta leading her flock through the sky. The audience murmured in admiration.

"This is Greta," Sarah continued. "She's not just a goose—she's a leader, a teacher, and a reminder of what we can achieve when we stop seeing wildlife as problems to solve and start seeing them as partners in a shared world."

The presentation detailed the sanctuary project, from its humble beginnings to its global impact. Sarah spoke about the drones, the no-fly zones, and the lessons learned from observing the geese.

"Our work is far from finished," Sarah concluded. "But Greta's flock has shown us the way. The sky is vast, and it can be a home for everyone—if we're willing to share it."

The room erupted in applause, the enthusiasm a testament to the power of Greta's story.

Back at the wetlands, Greta stood on the hill as the sun dipped below the horizon. The younger geese were playing in the pond, their laughter mingling with the rustling of reeds. Horace was telling stories to a group of goslings, his gruff voice softened by the joy of sharing wisdom.

Max sat beside Greta, his gaze fixed on the horizon. "Do you think the skies will always be this peaceful?" he asked.

Greta glanced at him, her expression thoughtful. "The skies are only as peaceful as we make them, Max. It's up to all of us—humans and geese—to protect them."

Max nodded, his determination evident. “I’ll help, Greta. I’ll do whatever it takes.”

Greta smiled, her heart swelling with pride. “I know you will, Max. And one day, you’ll lead the flock as I have.”

As the stars began to appear, Sarah and Tom arrived at the wetlands, their footsteps quiet on the soft earth. They watched from a distance as Greta and her flock settled in for the night, the scene a picture of harmony.

“She’s extraordinary,” Tom said softly. “I’ve never seen anything like her.”

Sarah nodded, her gaze fixed on Greta. “She’s more than extraordinary. She’s a reminder of what’s possible when we choose to listen, learn, and work together.”

As the night deepened, Greta stood watch over the wetlands, her heart filled with a sense of accomplishment and hope. The journey had been long and fraught with challenges, but it had also been rich with lessons and triumphs.

And as she looked up at the star-filled sky, Greta knew that her legacy wasn’t just in the sanctuary or the flock. It was in the bond that had formed between two worlds, in the belief that the sky truly belonged to all.

THE END

www.ingramcontent.com/pod-product-compliance
Ingram Content Group UK Ltd.
Pitfield, Milton Keynes, MK11 3LW, UK
UKHW022121211224
452733UK00012B/730

9 798230 296423